MW01703430

CAN'T ESCAPE

(A Nora Price Mystery—Book 3)

Kate Bold

Kate Bold

Bestselling author Kate Bold is author of the ALEXA CHASE SUSPENSE THRILLER series, comprising six books (and counting); the ASHLEY HOPE SUSPENSE THRILLER series, comprising six books (and counting); the CAMILLE GRACE FBI SUSPENSE THRILLER series, comprising eight books (and counting); the HARLEY COLE FBI SUSPENSE THRILLER series, comprising eleven books (and counting); the KAYLIE BROOKS PSYCHOLOGICAL SUSPENSE THRILLER series, comprising five books (and counting); the EVE HOPE FBI SUSPENSE THRILLER series, comprising seven books (and counting); the DYLAN FIRST FBI SUSPENSE THRILLER series, comprising five books (and counting); the LAUREN LAMB FBI SUSPENSE THRILLER series, comprising five books (and counting); the KELSEY HAWK MYSTERY series, comprising five books (and counting); the NORA PRICE MYSTERY series, comprising five books (and counting); and the NINA VEIL MYSTERY series, comprising five books (and counting).

An avid reader and lifelong fan of the mystery and thriller genres, Kate loves to hear from you, so please feel free to visit www.kateboldauthor.com to learn more and stay in touch.

ISBN: 978-1-0943-9695-8

BOOKS BY KATE BOLD

NINA VEIL MYSTERY
AWAY FROM HERE (Book #1)
AWAY FROM HIM (Book #2)
AWAY FROM HOPE (Book #3)
AWAY FROM HOME (Book #4)
AWAY FROM HUMANITY (Book #5)

NORA PRICE MYSTERY
CAN'T RUN (Book #1)
CAN'T HIDE (Book #2)
CAN'T ESCAPE (Book #3)
CAN'T SLEEP (Book #4)
CAN'T FORGET (Book #5)

KELSEY HAWK MYSTERY
DEAD INSIDE (Book #1)
DEAD RECKONING (Book #2)
DEAD TO ME (Book #3)
DEAD SILENCE (Book #4)
DEAD TO DAWN (Book #5)

ALEXA CHASE SUSPENSE THRILLER
THE KILLING GAME (Book #1)
THE KILLING TIDE (Book #2)
THE KILLING HOUR (Book #3)
THE KILLING POINT (Book #4)
THE KILLING FOG (Book #5)
THE KILLING PLACE (Book #6)

ASHLEY HOPE SUSPENSE THRILLER
LET ME GO (Book #1)
LET ME OUT (Book #2)
LET ME LIVE (Book #3)
LET ME BREATHE (Book #4)

LET ME FORGET (Book #5)
LET ME ESCAPE (Book #6)

CAMILLE GRACE FBI SUSPENSE THRILLER
NOT ME (Book #1)
NOT NOW (Book #2)
NOT WELL (Book #3)
NOT HER (Book #4)
NOT NORMAL (Book #5)
NOT AGAIN (Book #6)
NOT SAFE (Book #7)
NOT TODAY (Book #8)

HARLEY COLE FBI SUSPENSE THRILLER
NOWHERE SAFE (Book #1)
NOWHERE LEFT (Book #2)
NOWHERE TO RUN (Book #3)
NOWHERE LIKE THIS (Book #4)
NOWHERE GIRL (Book #5)
NOWHERE TO HIDE (Book #6)
NOWHERE CERTAIN (Book #7)
NOWHERE PURE (Book #8)
NOWHERE SOUND (Book #9)
NOWHERE SANE (Book #10)
NOWHERE TRUE (Book #11)

KAYLIE BROOKS PYSCHOLOGICAL SUSPENSE THRILLER
LAST BREATH (Book #1)
LAST CHANCE (Book #2)
LAST WISH (Book #3)
LAST SHOT (Book #4)
LAST MISTAKE (Book #5)

EVE HOPE FBI SUSPENSE THRILLER
IN HIS BLOOD (Book #1)
IN HIS SIGHTS (Book #2)
IN HIS REACH (Book #3)
IN HIS MIND (Book #4)
IN HIS WAY (Book #5)

IN HIS THOUGHTS (Book #6)
IN HIS DREAMS (Book #7)

DYLAN FIRST FBI SUSPENSE THRILLER
OUT OF REACH (Book #1)
OUT OF TOUCH (Book #2)
OUT OF TIME (Book #3)
OUT OF BOUNDS (Book #4)
OUT OF LUCK (Book #5)

LAUREN LAMB FBI SUSPENSE THRILLER
SOMETHING KNOCKING (Book #1)
SOMETHING CALLING (Book #2)
SOMETHING WRONG (Book 3)
SOMETHING DARK (Book #4)
SOMETHING TO HIDE (Book #5)

PROLOGUE

Not again . . .

Keith Thayer hated when the security alarms were triggered at one of the six abandoned buildings his firm monitored. It meant that he'd have to leave his cozy basement office to check out the situation personally. As the autumn season approached, the temperatures late at night and early in the morning were the coldest, and he hated the cold.

However, he didn't have much of a choice. They were short-staffed, and none of the empty buildings had onsite security personnel. It was a cost-savings his company offered, but it was also a pain when things like this happened.

He sighed as he pulled up outside the dilapidated, darkened Newell Auto Shop, rural Blackburn County, Massachusetts' only automotive body shops. He didn't see any immediate signs of a break-in.

Another false alarm, I hope.

Keith had never worked "in the field" before. He wasn't a former military or a retired cop. He didn't have a license to carry a concealed weapon like some of the other guys, and probably couldn't shoot a gun if he wanted to. and he wasn't sure if his tire iron was still in the trunk.

What are you going to do if there's someone inside?

Keith shook the thought from his mind. There was no time to panic. He had work to do.

He locked his car and did his best to march as confidently as possible to the partially boarded up glass door. He hoped if anyone was inside and they saw him coming, they'd be at least a little intimidated.

Keith pulled the ring of keys from his pocket and tried each key until the lock clicked. He never could remember which key went where. He tapped the flashlight app on his phone and held it in front of him as he tentatively walked into the deserted building.

"Security! If anyone's here, now's the time to show yourself," he called out into the darkness, doing his best to sound big and boisterous, although he was neither.

The light swept across the floor, illuminating piles of snapped boards and broken tiles. The place had never been very orderly. Each step into the building grew more and more precarious. He knew the general layout of the place, but he could not remember where the service bays were. He felt certain he'd seen a couple of garage doors out front, which could be for storage or service.

Just as he shined the light back in front of him, he caught himself before he stepped straight into an open pit.

That would've hurt, he thought, skirting around it.

Keith arced the light off to the left and then to the right to identify the perimeter of the service bay carved into the floor. He noticed some stairs against one of the walls off to the right that appeared to go down into the service bay.

"If anyone's down there, now's your chance to get out of here," he bellowed. Then, he listened to the darkness and waited to see if he heard anything moving anywhere around him.

When only silence answered him, Keith made his way over to the stairs and cautiously made his way down. Nerves jittered through him as if he'd drank too many cups of coffee, and he shoved his phone out in front of him to light his way.

Cobwebs draped like ghostly curtains across the old hooks where greasy tools used to hang on the walls. A faint metallic tang lingered in the air, no doubt an aromatic stain from the countless repairs performed within these walls. Keith didn't like empty buildings. They had too many secrets.

Once he reached the bottom of the stairs, he moved the light around the area. There wasn't much to see other than an old, rusted tool storage chest with open drawers and a broken wheel. He hurried across the open space to a narrow hallway.

Keith found a door cracked open with a foul odor emanating from the inside. He quickly held his nose with his free hand and confirmed with the flashlight the door led to a bathroom. He realized it suddenly didn't seem as dark as it had on the other side of the service bay or upstairs.

He clicked off his flashlight. There was pale light emanating from another room about ten steps ahead of him. He could not recall if there was another service bay, or if the room was an office.

The hallway was narrow, with another door on the right. He tried the knob, but it was locked. Keith did his best to keep his footfalls soft, just in case he was about to surprise a squatter.

"Security!" he shouted as he neared the opening to the room, hoping if there was someone to catch, they'd flee from the sound.

As Keith crossed the threshold of a smaller service bay, he was suddenly paralyzed by the scene in front of him. His eyes darted to the side and back again. It was like a piece of artwork, staged there, just for him.

And yet, this "artwork" was not pretty in the least. It was eerie, macabre. He stood there, still, trying to process. It was as if an icy grip had seized his heart, stealing his breath and electrifying him at the same time.

A portable work light with neon casing sat off to the side, the light dim as if its battery was running down. In front of the work light was tapered, slender, four-sided pillar. It reminded him a lot of the Washington Monument, only it was about three feet tall.

The object looked heavy, like it could be made of concrete or stone. Keith's eyes followed the long shadow it cast to where the slumped form of a man laid. There was something unnatural with how the man was positioned, but Keith didn't want to get too close to find out what was wrong.

He heard his phone clank on the ground before he realized he'd dropped it.

He kept his eyes fastened to the man's body, terrified that any moment the person was going to jump up and attack him. Keith reached down and patted the ground until he found his phone, his heartbeat slamming double-time in his ears.

Once he had his phone in hand, he lurched back and darted towards the other side of the auto body shop, desperate to escape. He fumbled over a couple of boards but regained his footing enough to make it to the stairs. Keith scrambled up the stairs, practically on all fours, racing to get out of the service bay area as quickly as possible.

As he made it to the top of the stairs, he double-clicked the side button on his phone to make the flashlight come on again. At that moment, he heard a sound.

Someone else is here.

Heart in his throat, he bolted across the creaky floor and out the door without a single look back.

Keith hurried to his car, locking the doors as soon as he was safe inside. He struggled to catch his breath, his lungs burning from exertion and lack of oxygen. Rapid, shallow breaths were all he could manage, but they weren't cutting it. Keith's heart was banging so hard in his chest he was sure it was going to burst out of it like an alien creature.

He closed his eyes and forced himself to slow down his breathing. He was safe. No one was after him. He had to calm down so he could call the cops.

Deep breath in. Hold. And let it go.

Keith repeated the mantra in his head a few times until he was finally breathing normally again. His heartbeat steadied, the feeling in his fingers returned enough so he could use them to call 9-1-1.

When the operator answered, he could only manage a single word. "Help."

CHAPTER ONE

Nora Price drove slowly up the gravel drive to the overgrown lot where the abandoned ranch house sat rotting, waiting for time to tear it down.

Here, again.

She couldn't fight the feeling that she'd missed something the first time.

The file she'd discovered on the Samantha Banks' abduction had listed this house as the address where the girl had been kept. The case had been eerily similar to her and her sister's abductions. Samantha Banks had been walking home after work one evening when she disappeared, just like Nora and Sophia. She'd escaped after a few days – also like Nora – but the only thing the girl could remember was that she'd been kept in an attic.

At least she had some idea of where she'd been kept, Nora thought as she stared up at the house.

More than a decade earlier, Nora and her sister, Sophia, had locked up JP's Diner in a hurry after their shift. They'd taken a shortcut through the woods so Sophia would not be late for cheerleading practice. It wasn't their usual route, but they were rushing and didn't see what lurked in the trees and shadows around them. At least, not until it was too late.

Like Samantha, Nora didn't remember much, either, not even where they'd been taken or by whom. But she did remember walking behind her sister, watching Sophia's blonde ponytail swish back and forth, irritated at the very fact that they were even sisters. Everyone loved Sophia. She was the bright, shining star that everyone wanted to know.

Even the bad guys.

Nora had been a drab and brooding teen with no light to call her own. She often thought of herself as the moon and Sophia as the sun.

Her parents had fawned over Sophia. No one cared about the moon when the sun was out.

Even now, Nora had a rocky relationship with her parents, her father, especially. After Sophia disappeared, they hadn't simply transferred the love they once showered upon Sophia to her. No, instead, her father became moody and prone to rage-filled outbursts. Her mother had withdrawn.

Nora had gotten out, yes. But rather than celebrate it, they wondered how she could possibly leave Sophia behind.

The answer, of course, was easy. She had had no other choice.

Her heart shuddered at the fractured memory of the escape. It had been chaos. After she'd somehow gotten free, the next thing Nora knew, she was running through a dark forest, branches and thorns grabbing at her arms and legs like they were desperate to catch her and hold her hostage. She didn't know where she'd been. She didn't know what had happened or who had taken them. She didn't know where Sophia was. She didn't know anything. Nora was alone, and Sophia was just... gone.

And even now, she couldn't help feeling that her parents blamed her. They assumed she was gone forever. It was like a permanent eclipse had settled upon their lives. But Nora refused to accept it. She could not imagine her world without Sophia, just like she could not imagine a world without the sun.

Now, as she stepped out of the car, she said a little prayer for even the smallest of clues. *Please. Let this second time be a charm.*

She'd hoped the abandoned house would jolt the mangled pieces of her memory loose until something finally fell into place. She didn't have any other leads, so this had seemed like a good place to start. She'd checked out the house, searching it from top to bottom to find something that would connect Samantha Banks' story to her own.

But there hadn't been anything there to find.

Like the rest of the house, the attic had been decrepit and covered in cobwebs. But there was no sign anything untoward had happened in that place except for a dead squirrel decomposing in the grate. Nora had thought for sure Samantha Banks had gotten it wrong.

Then, she'd thought about it and wondered if maybe the girl hadn't been kept in the attic after all. Maybe she'd been kept in the basement of the house and remembered it wrong. Nora shuddered every time she even thought of the word *basement*, much less went near one. Maybe her incessant fear was some sort of clue about where she'd been kept with her sister all those years ago.

Nora had scoured the old house, but there was no basement. Not even a crawl space. When she'd realized the house sat on a concrete slab, she'd even started to wonder if she was losing her mind.

What was the point of this lead if it hadn't led her anywhere? She was so tired of spinning her wheels, trying to make connections her mind had somehow forgotten. It was exhausting.

After her last case, where nothing was as it seemed, Nora had made the decision to come back to the abandoned ranch house one more time. Maybe she'd missed something.

So here she was. Again.

Something about this old house just didn't fit. Nora picked up the thin manila file on her passenger seat and flipped through the few pages it contained.

Samantha Banks had been found wandering on the side of the road less than a hundred feet from the ranch house. She was disoriented, dehydrated, and didn't even know her own name. A driver passing by had noticed the girl was barefoot and seemed lost. It had been a cold night, too cold for no shoes or socks, so they'd stopped to help. When the driver approached the girl, she'd begun screaming in terror for help.

The driver had given their statement and said they thought the girl had been coming from the ranch house based on the direction she'd been walking. The police checked it out, but they didn't find anything other than the abandoned old home.

Nora pulled out Samantha's statement and read it again. Her eyes caught on a word and widened.

He kept me in the dark. Somewhere dark and quiet, an attic.

Maybe Samantha Banks didn't actually know that it was the attic where she'd been kept. The police had just assumed the ranch house was the spot because of the eyewitness who had found her, but maybe she'd been kept somewhere else. Somewhere nearby.

Nora scanned the area and sighed, frustrated at the lack of police work done on the case. She remembered the case of Miranda Forster, another kidnapped women who had miraculously escaped, who had told her the place she'd been held had been shoddy. She closed the file and walked a little ways down the road, which looked to be a dead-end street. There was only one other structure at the beginning of the street, and it had looked abandoned, too.

Nora put her car back in gear and drove slowly down the road towards the falling-down mess of a building she'd spotted earlier. She parked out front and looked around. The roof had caved in some time ago, and it looked like no one had set foot on even the lawn in ages.

Maybe decades, she thought.

There were hot spots in the yard where the heat of summer had burned the life out of the grass. In other spots, weeds sprouted to new heights, reaching towards the sky and anyone who dared to come near. The land was barren in comparison to the old ranch house down the street, which could barely be seen from the road because of all the overgrowth.

Nora could tell the building wasn't a house or any kind of domicile based on the structure. It looked like it maybe could have been an old town hall building, but that didn't make any sense. Aside from the old ranch house, there were no other buildings or even remnants of buildings for miles. This was the most rural part of Blackburn County, Massachusetts, an area about 100 miles to the west of Boston, close to the Berkshires. She doubted there'd ever been much here beyond the two buildings and empty fields.

She walked around the perimeter of the building, trying to figure out if there was a way in. It didn't exactly seem safe, given the roof's collapse. Large swaths of plywood were nailed over what Nora presumed were windows. However, the front entrance was tidy and clean, as if it had been used only minutes before her arrival. She wasn't sure if the place was steady enough for her to go inside and check it out, but her curiosity burned too hot for her to ignore it.

Nora trekked back to the front of the building and started towards the front door. She tentatively climbed the stairs, stopping abruptly on the third step when a flicker of movement caught her eye off to the right. She turned her head just in time to see a shock of white disappear through a half-covered opening.

She rushed down the stairs and crouched down to peer into the darkened spacc. Nora pulled out her phone and tapped the flashlight app. She shined it into the black hole. Her eyes could not make out much except a pair of frightened glowing eyes peering back at her. Suddenly, the animal hissed at her, making her jump at the unexpected noise. Then, it disappeared into the darkness.

Nothing but a cat.

Nora sighed deeply before laughing at herself. Something about this place gave her the creeps, put her on guard more than usual.

Maybe that's a good thing.

Suddenly, an image of her sister's wide, bright smile flashed in her mind. Maybe the cat was her sign to keep going. Nora wasn't sure she believed in signs anymore, but she knew she needed to find her way inside this building, into the shadows that lurked beneath it.

Nora walked around the building again and could not find another entrance from the outside. So she decided to return to the front and marched straight up the stairs to the door. Her chest tightened as she tried the knob.

What might be lurking on the other side of the door?

The door popped open like it had been waiting for her. Part of the structure was exposed by the gaping hole where the roof had once been, while the edges remained in shadow. Nora turned the flashlight on her phone on again, using it as a guide for her footing.

The space that sprawled out before her was expansive, some kind of meeting space or conference room. There were no fragments of the past left behind, nothing for her to piece together and help her figure out what kind of place this used to be.

Is there where he kept Samantha Banks? Is this where he kept us?

Nora could not help conflating Samantha Banks' kidnapping with her own. They felt the same even though they weren't. She shook the thought from her mind and forced herself to focus.

Each step was timid, uncertain of how sturdy the ground beneath her feet was. Nora swept the space with the light, searching for doors or hallways – something, anything, that would lead her down below, to wherever the cat had been.

At first, she didn't see anything. Just like the old, abandoned ranch house. Then, the light caught a piece of metal in the farthest corner of the left side of the room. She made her way over and realized there was a hatch in the floor.

Nora stood above the hatch, her knees trembling at the thought of what lay beneath her. She was terrified to look, to keep going, but she knew turning back was no longer an option. She bent down, grasped the handle, and yanked the hatch up.

A cloud of dust billowed out around her as she flipped the hatchback. Nora shined the light down and saw narrow steps descending into the darkness.

Just like hell.

Nora took a deep breath and carefully took one step at a time until she disappeared below the floor. The temperature of the air cooled around her, and instantly she knew she was in some kind of basement.

Her muscles tightened and she felt like her hearing was suddenly amplified. Every noise, every sound grabbed her attention. Her palms dampened with perspiration, and her mouth dried up like the Sahara. A chill ran down her spine at the thought, and all Nora wanted to do was run back up the stairs and never come back.

Instead, she forced herself deeper into the darkness, just like she had with Dr. Eldridge and his hypnotherapy. Nora knew now the answers were in the dark, and no matter how afraid she was, she had to keep going.

As the light swept across the room, Nora started to see anomalies, things that didn't make sense. Deep grooves carved into the concrete floor like someone had moved something heavy without picking it up. Rough holes in the cinderblocks, like someone had driven large spikes into the walls to secure things like chains and manacles.

The more she looked, the less she understood. It was like seeing all the pieces of a puzzle but not being able to see the picture they made. All she had to go on was how she felt. And how she felt was that terrible things had happened in this place.

Maybe the same terrible things had happened to *her*. Nora wasn't sure she actually recognized the place, but she could feel the horror that'd happened here. She could feel *him*, and she knew in her gut that he had operated here.

But was this where her own horrors had taken place, or not?

As Nora looked around, desperate to find something familiar, the space seemed to get smaller and smaller. It was like she was dreaming, but she knew she wasn't. Her breath caught as the light reached out in front of her, highlighting the wall below the stairs.

There, illuminated like a beacon in the darkness, was an old, hand-carved wooden cross with frayed edges, hanging there like it had been waiting just for her.

CHAPTER TWO

Nora took a quick sip of her club soda and smiled at Dane, excited to see him, but even more excited to tell him what she'd discovered.

"I was so frustrated when I checked out the site and there wasn't any basement. I felt like I was missing something. Turned out, I was."

"Do you think it was the same guy who did those things to you?" Dane asked, looking up from his club sandwich. They'd been planning to go to dinner, but they'd had to settle on lunch when they could not get their schedules to align for any other time of day.

"I don't know."

Nora didn't care if it was lunch, coffee, or just sitting on a park bench together. She was just happy to see his warm brown eyes again. When she looked at him, something settled within her that she didn't even know had been disturbed.

She wasn't sure if they were officially dating or still getting to know one another, but she liked it whatever it was, regardless of the label. Dane was someone she'd instantly felt safe with, like nothing bad could ever happen to her when she was with him. It was intoxicating, and she could not get enough, especially because Nora could not remember the last time she truly felt – or was – safe.

"So how did you find this place?" he asked, confused.

"After I looked through the witness statements, I realized the victim never identified exactly where she'd been. All that trauma . . .it was easy to get confused. She'd thought it was an attic, but I don't think it actually *was* an attic."

"Gotcha."

"So I checked out this run-down building that was like half a mile away from the house, and sure enough, it's a basement."

"Lots of places have basements, Nora," Dane said flatly, like he didn't understand the magnitude of her discovery.

"No, I know. But *this* place is a *church* and it has a basement," she smiled proudly, waiting for him to get it.

Except he didn't. Dane just kept eating his sandwich, almost like he hadn't even heard what she'd said.

"In my hypnotherapy session, I saw that the place we'd been kept was a church basement. *This* is a church basement," she said, emphasizing every syllable as if to stress the importance of what she was saying. "It could be where it happened."

"Nora, we go to group therapy in a church basement, too. I'll agree, it's a connection, but if the place was abandoned, anyone could've just been squatting there, right?" he asked. His tone was innocent, but his words challenged her in a way she hadn't expected.

Sometimes, he seemed to be so engaged, so interested in everything she had to say. But, for whatever reason, today, he was acting completely different. She could not tell what the catalyst for the changed behavior was, but she didn't like it.

"No. I could tell, Dane. This wasn't just *any* old church basement. Terrible things had happened there. It was terrible, and there were things on the walls. If you'd seen it, you'd understand," she huffed.

"I'm sure you're right," he nodded as he refocused on his sandwich. Something was off. Dane seemed more distant than usual. It was a side of him she hadn't seen before, and she didn't really know how to handle it.

"Well, anyway, I'm not really sure what to do next. I looked into that church, and it was abandoned since before I was kidnapped. So it's not like I could look into members of the congregation. And if it isn't the place where it happened, it's not like I can look into every abandoned church in the area. And let's say I did, let's say I tried to follow up on every congregation member out there. It had taken forever, and I probably would just end up back where I started. As much as I'd love to dive in headfirst, I know I'd just be searching for a blonde hair in field of wheat."

Part of her wanted him to encourage her, to tell her it was worth pursuing. But he didn't.

"True. And you still have your day job to consider. It would be hard to fit all that in and still be in the FBI," he agreed.

Nora sighed. Did he understand how important this was to her? She took another sip of her drink. She wasn't sure how to respond to his lack of interest and aloof behavior. Should she confront him? Was he already bored with her and her incessant rambling about her trauma? Did she do something wrong?

His disinterest overwhelmed her. It wasn't normal. But then again, it's not like they'd spent hours and hours together. Maybe this *was* his normal, and she just didn't know it. Now that they were more comfortable together, his true nature was coming through. Nora tried to stifle the unending questions whirling through her brain like a tornado, but then one burst through.

"Dane, is something going on?"

"What do you mean?" he asked as he looked up at her. His brown eyes didn't seem so warm anymore. They weren't unkind, but they weren't present either.

"You seem kind of distracted."

He looked down at the crust of his sandwich. "Do I?"

"Yes, you do."

"Oh. I guess I didn't realize," he said. It was full of regret, but she noticed he wasn't actually saying he was sorry.

"Well, I just want you to know that even though I've been rambling on about all this other stuff, I'm not some self-involved maniac who doesn't care what's going on with you. We don't have to just talk about me," she said, forcing a smile she hoped would be more welcoming than desperate.

Because she felt desperate, like she was losing him.

"Oh, no, it's just... I have a lot on my mind at the moment. Nothing you need to worry about."

"Okay, but you know you can talk to me about anything, right?"

"I do, but this is just... it's just stuff I have to deal with. There's no point in burdening you with my troubles on top of everything else going on. I can handle it," he said with a tight smile, but it seemed like a halfhearted attempt to reassure her.

"It's not a burden. I promise. Just like I hope I'm not burdening you," she said, hopeful and terrified at the same time.

"You're not. It's fine. Really, Nora. Everything's fine," he assured her.

"Okay, but you'll tell me if it isn't. Right?"

Instead of answering her, offering more reassurance, Dane half-shrugged with a nod. She wasn't sure if he was actually agreeing to talk to her, or if he was just placating her.

Nora frowned. It was still too early in their relationship for her to put pressure on him to talk about stuff if he wasn't ready to talk about it. She knew he had his own demons, ones he was working to overcome. They'd met at a meeting for trauma sufferers, after all. But he was reluctant to speak about his past, and she didn't push. If Dane didn't want to talk to her about whatever was going on with him, then she shouldn't force him. She knew not everyone was ready to rehash their tragedies like she was, and even had days – years – where she wasn't always in the mood to do so.

Nora finished up the rest of her chips in silence, which Dane didn't seem to mind or notice. She hoped this was just a one-off and not the beginning of the end. She really liked Dane, and she wasn't ready for them to call it quits just yet.

But she had to wonder . . . was *he*?

CHAPTER THREE

Nora had planned to hang out with Dane after lunch until it was time for their group therapy session, but as they stood up to leave the restaurant, he told her he had errands to run and would meet her at the church later.

Then he made a quick exit without even giving her a kiss on the cheek. Not even a wave. He just vanished, quick as he could, separating from her as if she was diseased.

She was disappointed, but not entirely surprised, considering how preoccupied he'd been at lunch.

She stared at the empty journal page in front of her. At last week's session, they'd talked about how journaling could help process trauma and the emotions associated with it. Cora, the group leader, had gone out of her way to share the benefits of journaling, from providing a private outlet for emotions to organizing thoughts and memories. It had been a while since she'd attempted to do any journaling, so she figured it wouldn't hurt to try.

Nora had never been interested in writing, much less writing about what happened to her and Sophia. Her parents had always encouraged her to try to forget. Besides, it didn't make sense to her to try and write about something she didn't actually remember.

Dr. Eldridge had also encouraged her to write down anything she remembered from their hypnotherapy sessions. They were recorded, but he'd told her it was important to capture whatever she was thinking and feeling about any resurfacing memories. He'd also said journaling could help her identify triggers for her nightmares and possible coping mechanisms. The only problem was she could never remember enough to even fill a page.

Instead of writing about her or her sister's abductions, Nora decided to make some notes about what she saw in the abandoned church and some of the things she needed to check out further. She knew it was a church, but *what kind* of church, what denomination? When was it last a functional building? Who had all the owners been over the years? She'd have to research it more to see if she could make any connections to her own case.

The kidnapper was likely not dumb enough to put his name on the record somewhere, but maybe one of the previous owners knew him. Maybe he was someone connected to the building. There was definitely more to explore, she could feel it.

Her phone buzzed in her pocket, snapping her out of her question spiral. She hesitated when she didn't recognize the number. At the last minute, she answered.

"Hello?"

"Hi, it's Cora from the Wendy's Hope group. Do you have a minute?" the woman asked, her voice warm and soothing as always.

"Of course. I was just jotting some thoughts down in my journal. What's up?"

"I've been making the rounds this afternoon, and I'm afraid I have some sad news to share. We have quite a few new members, so I didn't want to announce this at the session this afternoon."

"Okay..." Nora faltered. She wasn't sure she wanted to know with this kind of lead up.

"I'm sorry to tell you that I learned this morning that Trudie Whittier died from suicide late last night."

Nora's heart sank into her stomach and then felt like it kept falling. She knew Trudie. The woman had been a staple at every meeting, sharing her harrowing story with a strength Nora could not imagine ever having.

"I can't believe it... she seemed like she was doing so well..." Nora muttered, still processing what the group leader had just told her.

"I know. We're all completely still in shock."

"So the others know? Are we still meeting later?"

Nora expected the woman would say they were canceling the session. She could not imagine sitting in the room after a bomb like this had been sct off. This was a terrible trigger for all of them: trauma on top of trauma.

"Yes, most of the others know. Those I've been able to get a hold of anyway. And yes, we still have a session later. I think in times like these, coming together is more important than ever. And please always keep in mind, the sessions are optional. You're always welcome, Nora, but you should always take into consideration how you're feeling first. I do hope you'll join us, though."

"Yeah," Nora agreed, although her brain wasn't sure it was on board with the words coming out of her mouth. "I'll be there."

"Let me know if you need anything. Otherwise, I'll see you in a bit."

Nora said goodbye and disconnected the call. She was glad she was already sitting down. The news of Trudie's death was like a one-two punch to the gut.

Trudie Whittier's story was one of the first Nora had heard when she started coming to the sessions. She'd been in a horribly abusive relationship where trips to the emergency room had become a weekly occurrence. After her daughter was born, though, that had been the motivation she needed to finally get away from her husband. She saved up enough money to leave him and made a plan to get out. Except he somehow found out about her plan and came home early to confront her.

Trudie didn't remember what had happened next. It had been too traumatic, too terrible. Eventually, the police and the lawyers filled her in.

Trudie's husband had brutally attacked his wife, beating her so savagely her blood had been found all over the house like some kind of horror movie had been filmed there. Then, as if that hadn't been horrific enough, the man killed their daughter, an innocent little girl who had never done anything but love the man.

It was always at this part of the story that Trudie had struggled the most. Riddled with guilt over her death, she never said her daughter's name when she talked about what had happened to them. It was like her name was too sacred to live in that space of trauma and pain.

Trudie was in a coma for five months. When she woke up, she had no recollection of what had happened to her or her family. The only good thing that had come out of the whole experience was that her husband had died in a shootout with the cops. Trudie admitted every time she talked about her experience that she wished he hadn't gotten off so easily.

Most of the time, when Trudie told the group, she was stoic until she got to the part about her daughter. Only then, it seemed, would she allow the emotions in. Her voice would crack, tears would stream out of the corners of her eyes, but she'd always push through.

The cruelty she'd suffered was unimaginable, but she never shied away from sharing her journey with the others. Every time she spoke, she'd say she believed she'd survived so she could help others learn from her mistakes. She'd always emphasized how important it was to her to talk about the abuse she'd experienced, the way he'd beg her to forgive him, only to hurt her even worse the next time around.

Nora wondered what could've possibly changed that made Trudie unable to see how important her story was and how so many people needed to still hear it. She'd been such a tireless advocate for domestic violence awareness, marching with other victims of abuse and calling on government officials to do more. What could've happened to make all of that conviction go away seemingly overnight?

Nora wasn't sure she still wanted to go to group. It was no doubt going to be a grim atmosphere to walk into, much less sit through for an hour. She weighed the pros and cons of skipping the session and ultimately decided it was important to go. Her mom and Dane would likely be there, so she felt like it was important for her to go too. In her own way, Nora wanted to honor Trudie for everything she'd tried to do. She'd deserved better. The one thing that gave Nora some peace of mind was imagining Trudie finally being reunited with her daughter.

*

Nora arrived early and sat near the back as usual. She kept an eye out on the entrance for Dane and her mom as people began to file in. She noticed no one was smiling as they arrived, which wasn't a surprise. But now, everyone seemed almost shellshocked, too. The sadness of Trudie's death filled the space long before all the seats were filled.

When the meeting began, an older man with salt-and-pepper hair and matching beard stepped to the front of the group. He wore a dark navy suit and resigned expression, one Nora had seen too many times before at memorial services and funerals.

"Hello, everyone. My name is Pastor Patrick Ellis, and I'm the pastor here at the First Baptist Church. We are so proud to host the Wendy's Hope group sessions, and we're grateful you all are able to come together in a safe place to work through the hardships and turmoil you've faced in your lives."

Nora looked around the room for Dane or her mom. She didn't see either of them. People shifted uncomfortably in their seats as the pastor spoke, especially those who had expressed any uneasiness about religion in previous sessions.

Wendy's Hope had victims of all types of trauma. Nora had heard stories from others who had been in similarly abusive relationships like Trudie. She'd heard others share their experiences as victims of random acts of violence, while others talked about suffering at the hands of cult-like or religious leaders. Everyone's trauma was unique and personal to them, but they were united under one thing. It was a struggle to walk through the door and seek healing, no matter what had happened in the past.

As she sat there, her eyes caught on the cross above the pastor's head. Her own kidnapping, in a church. She'd been here before, and yet it hadn't rattled any memories loose. Why had she never made that connection to the church basement before?

Now, she was even less excited about the meeting, much less having a pastor trying to console them over something that would not – could not – ever make sense. Trudie had seemed like she was the strongest of them all, and in the end, she wasn't.

What does that mean for the rest of us?

"I wanted to speak for a moment today because Trudie Whittier was not only a member of Wendy's Hope, but also a steadfast member of our congregation. While we may never understand why she was called home so soon, we understand some wounds are harder to heal than others. We also consider each of you a part of our community, and we wanted to extend our most heartfelt condolences over our dear Trudie's passing. Please do not hesitate to reach out if you need support of any kind. Cora is a wonderful leader, and we just wanted you to know you have us church folk here to support you as well."

The pastor stepped aside, and Cora began to talk about grief and the different support options available outside of Wendy's Hope and the church. Nora looked around again to see if maybe her mom or Dane had finally arrived, but neither of them were anywhere to be found.

At that moment, it hit her. Maybe Dane had heard about Trudie.

Was that what Dane had been brooding about earlier?

If it was, why wouldn't he have said something to her?

And her mother had been here, too. Trudie Whittier was someone she'd sat in the same room with, heard her story, maybe even spoken to at some point. Her mom would probably take the news pretty hard. While her parents remained mostly mum on the topic of Sophia, burying it deep within themselves, Nora's mother sobbed every time a celebrity she liked passed away. And those were people she didn't know personally.

Nora thought about calling, but instead she decided she'd ride by the house and see if her mom was home. She wanted to check in and make sure everything was okay.

As she walked to her car, Nora's phone buzzed in her pocket. It was a text from her partner, Jason Snyder.

We've got a case. Looks like a doozy. Meet me at the office in 20.

CHAPTER FOUR

In the office, Nora met her partner, Jason Snyder. He had a coffee waiting for her—black, just the way she liked it.

"Hey, you," he said, handing it to her. "You look like you need two of these."

"Maybe three." She yawned and lifted the lid to her nose, inhaling deeply. "What have we got?"

She had known Jason Snyder for almost six years. They'd met at the Academy and had become inseparable. He was her partner in crime fighting, her best friend, the only person in the world who always kept it real with her. He told her exactly what she needed to hear when she needed to hear it. It was one of her favorite things about him. That, and he was the easiest person in the world to be around. They always seemed to click.

Nora also loved that Jason had never handled her with kid gloves like everyone else. He knew about her past, but he didn't ever coddle her or pity her for it. It was just another thing about her, like the color of her eyes or her last name. He respected her boundaries, and he didn't push.

Jason was the one person she trusted the most and could tell anything to, although lately she hadn't been sharing as much with him as she usually did. Keeping some things to herself like her anxiety or panic attacks wasn't strange, but it was unusual she hadn't told him about Dane. Nora wasn't ready to answer questions about him, yet, or to try and explain their relationship.

Jason could smell B.S. a hundred miles away, and she knew he'd pick up on any insecurities she might have about Dane. They hadn't decided on any labels or defined things enough, she didn't know enough. It would never hold up under Jason's scrutiny, and Nora needed to believe it could be something real just for a little while longer.

She also hadn't told him about the dilapidated ranch house or the old, abandoned church. She wanted to, but it was mostly just hunches and theories, nothing concrete. Just like her memories. And it all was only coming together because of a hypnotherapy session Jason had already been skeptical about.

Nora felt in her bones that she was close to finding the man that'd ruined her and her family's lives. Maybe even close to finding Sophia. It was just a matter of time.

She waffled back and forth about telling Jason what she had so far. She could definitely use his perspective, but she hadn't decided if the narrative she was pulling together was strong enough to hold up under his scrutiny. This was the first possible lead she'd had in a long time, and she wasn't ready to see it fall apart like all the others.

Besides they had a new case and this one was definitely going to require their full attention. She read the case files with interest. So far, there were two victims. Both were found staged in isolated locations with small stone spires near the bodies. Other than those two details, they had nothing else in common.

It was too early to tell, it sounded like they'd stumbled upon another creep with a weird fetish. "Thrilling," she muttered, closing up the case file and getting ready to head out. "Is it just me or is this world getting sicker?"

Jason nodded. "It's not just you."

"I swear, every time I think I've heard it all . . ."

"I know what you mean. I'll drive," Jason announced as they stepped onto the elevator and she pushed the button for the garage level.

"Where are we headed, partner?" she asked.

She glared at him. He always wanted to drive, because in a small way, that gave him more control. Jason always kept her on her toes with how competitive he could be. Nora was pretty certain he was still irritated she'd graduated top of their class, and he was a distant second. He'd probably say *she* was the competitive one, but that wasn't true.

Nora was competitive with herself, not other people. She wanted to be her best, do her best, and if that meant she ended up besting others, so be it. She'd been like that even when she was little. She'd been on the swim team for seven years, and one of the reasons she'd loved it so much was because she could focus on besting herself, and usually that meant she'd win the race. Her drive for perfection made her a tough competitor, not any kind of desire for the sport of it.

Jason thrived on rivalry, which wasn't a bad thing. He loved the hunt, the thrill of a victory hard-won. It actually helped drive their partnership forward in a lot of ways. He was competing with her, and she was competing with herself. At the end of the day, they both won out.

"A town called Newell. It's about forty-five minutes away, on the northern end of Blackburn County. Ever hear of it?"

"I don't think so. Is it a legit town or like just a place on the map people collectively decided to call a town?" Nora smiled.

"Isn't that kind of the definition of a town, Nora?" he asked with a smirk.

"Yeah, yeah, whatever. Have *you* heard of Newell, Massachusetts?" she challenged.

"Not once," he laughed.

Nora loved how easy it was between them. He always knew exactly how to lighten things up, something she seemed incapable of doing on her own. Sure, they had their spats here and there, but they'd never had a serious fight in the almost-six years they'd known each other. The closest they'd gotten to something significant was on their last case, which to Nora was mostly just a big misunderstanding.

Since they had a long drive ahead of them, Nora decided to test the waters a little and talk to Jason about her session with Dr. Eldridge, the hypnotherapist. Maybe then she could gauge his reaction and decide how much else she wanted to share.

"So . . . I went to my hypnotherapy session," she began.

"Oh right, how did that go? Are you going to cluck like a chicken when you hear a whistle now?" he teased.

"I don't know. Why don't you whistle and find out?" she countered.

Jason smiled wide and then whistled two notes back-to-back – one high and one low. Nora froze for a millisecond, pulled her hands up to her armpits to make winged shapes and began to cluck. When she didn't stop, Jason's grin dissolved into slight panic.

"You are absolutely ridiculous if you think any second of that clucking was real," she said. "It's actually due to the brain damage I sustained when I was dropped on my head."

He smirked. "Funny," he said, as though it wasn't.

Well, he deserved it. Jason liked playing jokes on Nora. She remembered this one time when they were at the Academy, she'd lost her keys. She'd completely freaked out, which Jason had found hilarious. Then, as she ran around, searching everywhere, he'd randomly asked her if she knew if she'd been dropped on her head as a baby.

"What? Why are you asking me that?" she'd asked him.

"Well, I saw this thing on National Geographic where they were talking about how people who lose things a lot tended to be dropped on their heads as babies," he'd explained with a grin.

"Dr. Eldridge does not change people into poultry. He is a renowned hypnotherapist and doctor. Like the best in the country. He would not risk his license or reputation on a parlor trick, Jason," she scolded.

"You're right. I'm ridiculous. A regular man-child," he chided in agreement.

"Well, if you're quite finished making fun, I'll have you know the session was a wild success."

"A *wild* success, huh?" he asked, giving her side-eye.

"Let's be serious for a second, okay?" she asked, her tone instantly sobering the mood.

"Sure thing, Price. Lay it on me," he nodded as he watched the road. There wasn't any traffic, but she thought maybe he was just being careful. Sometimes he was hypervigilant, and other times he was reckless. Whenever she pointed out the inconsistency, he'd just shrug it off and say it was part of his charm.

"I remembered things, Jason," she said, her voice small.

"You did?" he asked, looking at her in surprise, and simultaneously almost swerving off the road.

"Watch the road, cowboy," she fussed.

"How much?" he asked as he swiped a quick look her way again, his interest piqued.

"A few things. Important things I never could remember before."

"Like what?" he pressed, his eagerness on full display.

"I know where he kept us now."

"Really?" he asked, shocked.

"Well, not the actual location on a map, but the type of place. An abandoned church basement."

"That tracks given how you tend to freeze up in basements," he nodded. Then, he added, "This is big, Nora. This could be a real lead after all these years."

"I know," she agreed, grateful he understood the magnitude of her news, unliked Dane had.

At that, his thoughts turned to her new flame. Nora could not help but wish Dane had been as interested in her discovery as Jason was. Jason had more history with her, so he'd had more opportunities to learn how and why something like this was important. But Dane had his own tragic backstory, something Jason didn't have, and yet, he hadn't seemed interested whatsoever in knowing more. Jason, on the other hand, was an enthusiastic listener, soaking in every word.

"And I think I might have also found one of the old churches he's used before."

"What? How?"

"Remember the Samantha Banks case I told you about? The file said she'd been kept in the attic, but I checked it out and there was no way. There was no trace anyone had been restrained in that place. It was just a regular old house."

"Wait, wasn't the victim the one who had said she'd been kept in the attic?" Jason asked, always keen to remember the details. It was yet another reason she appreciated his interest in what she was sharing. Because once she told him things, he never forgot them. It didn't matter how much time passed or what happened, he knew it like it had been his own history.

"That's what I thought, too! When I reread her statement, though, I realized it might not have been as concrete a statement as she'd thought," Nora said excitedly, unable to contain her enthusiasm. "There was no real follow-up on the question, so I started to think, what if she was just mistaken?"

"How in the world did no one go deeper into what she meant? That seems really... just poor policework on so many levels," he sighed.

"Yep. And the thing is that they just went off what the witness who had found her said, and for all they knew that *witness* could have been the kidnapper. Samantha Banks was too out of sorts to know up from down, much less if the person trying to supposedly help her had been the one who had taken her."

"That's wild."

"So, I retraced where Samantha had been found and there was this building not even a mile away. It was abandoned, too, with a collapsed roof, but it was close enough that she could have been walking from *there* and not the house."

"So of course you had to go into the creepy, crumbling building with a collapsed roof, Nora," Jason groaned. "Without your partner."

"Yes, but I was careful," she responded, hoping they weren't about to rehash their recent argument about how reckless she could be.

"Nora," he groaned again.

"I had to see for myself, Jason. And it's the place. It's an old church with a basement where people – or at least Samantha Banks – were chained to the walls."

Jason didn't respond. He didn't even look at her. Nora could not tell if he was trying to decide how to respond or if he was too mad to do so.

She waited to see if he'd say anything, but he just sat uncomfortably quiet next to her.

Nora could not handle silence. Ever since the kidnapping, she had to have noise or talking or something going on around her. A shrink told her it was probably related, but it didn't matter because Nora could not remember anything that had happened during that time. Another shrink agreed and said it reminded them of how birds would get quiet in the forest when larger prey was near.

Before she had a full-on meltdown, Nora spoke up.

"I'm sorry I didn't let you know what I was doing. I didn't want to make a big deal out of it until I knew there was something to make a big deal out of. You know how important this could be, and I just... I wanted to make sure before I got my hopes up," she tried to explain.

"It's fine, Nora," he sighed.

"You don't sound like it's fine," she countered.

"Well, it isn't, but... apologies only work the first time." He shrugged.

"What do you mean?"

"When you apologize for something and then you turn around and go out and do it again, it kind of makes the apology feel like it didn't mean anything. Like it was just a bunch of empty words you strung together to make the situation better or go away."

"That's not fair, Jason. My apologies are not empty," she defended.

"I'm not saying they are. I'm saying that's how it *feels*," he clarified.

“When I apologized to you after the whole Osmond Wright debacle, I meant every word.”

“And then you went out and put yourself in harm’s way without even a text? You’re the one who said you’d work on being reckless, Nora. *You* added that in. I didn’t force you to say it,” he said, his tone growing more heated than she’d expected.

“People make mistakes. It doesn’t mean their words don’t matter because they screw up,” she argued.

“Let’s agree to disagree before this turns into something bigger than it needs to be. Besides, we’re almost there,” he said, effectively shutting the argument down.

Part of the reason she and Jason had never had a full-on fight was because he’d usually do exactly what he was doing now. He’d shut it down and revisit it once he’d had some time to think about it. Sometimes, he’d apologize. Sometimes, the topic would never come up again. Nora knew that probably wasn’t the healthiest way to deal with conflict, but it seemed to work for them.

And it also would not do any good to try and argue her point when he got on his soap box. Jason had his convictions about certain things, and once he made up his mind, it was hard to change it. The best thing she could do was drop it.

She sighed, pulled out her phone, and clicked on the message app. She typed up a quick message to her mom, checking in to make sure she was okay after the news about Trudie Whittier.

Hi, Mom. I didn't see you at the group today. I just wanted to check in and make sure you're okay. I’m on a case, but I’ll call you later. Love you.

Nora tapped send. She looked over at Jason, expecting to find him back to his usual, jovial self, but instead found him steely-eyed, his jaw clenching over and over in aggravation. It was strange to see him getting so worked up. It’s not like anything happened to her. She was fine. She didn’t even have a scratch on her.

Nora started to say something, to try apologizing again, but decided against it. Jason needed time to cool down, to think through whatever was bothering him so much. Hopefully once they got to the crime scene, they could just focus on the case and get back into their natural working rhythm.

As the site pulled into view, she pocketed her phone and checked to make sure she had her gun on her. Whatever was going on with the men in her life, it would have to wait. They had a killer to find.

CHAPTER FIVE

Jason could never stay angry at Nora for long. By the time they'd arrived at the Newell Auto Shop, his frustration had dissipated. He pulled into a metered parking spot across from the crime scene and put the car in park.

"This place doesn't look like it's been open for business in a while," he commented. He notice the lettering on the front windows of the building were partially scratched off, so instead of saying "Newell Auto Shop", it said "Ne w l Au o hop".

"Do you know who our contact is?" Nora asked, her tone professional and clipped, which caught him off guard.

What does she have to be irritated about?

Neither one of them had said a word the last ten minutes of the drive. Jason had started to say something, to try and break the ice, but he noticed Nora seemed distracted, anxious. She kept checking her phone every few minutes. He wasn't sure if she was waiting on a call or text or if she was checking to see how much longer she had to be in the car with him.

Jason didn't want there to be tension between them, but he also wasn't going to be the first to apologize this time. He'd always been the one to say sorry first, even when he hadn't done anything wrong. And when it *was* his fault, he did everything he could to not make the same mistake twice.

Nora had been a risk taker for as long as he'd known her, but lately, it was more than that. The last two cases they'd worked had been especially hard, and Nora had put herself directly in harm's way with both suspects. It was getting dangerous. She was taking risks she didn't have to take.

Sometimes, those risks were part of the job. For example, driving fast while chasing a suspect through traffic was a risk. But it was a *calculated* risk, one where the pros and cons were supposed to have been carefully thought through.

That wasn't the type of risk Nora took. Instead, it was like she was playing a game of Russian Roulette, and Jason was just supposed to stand by and watch, hoping the chamber was still empty when she pulled the trigger again. There were only so many empty chambers to go before she got to the real bullet.

The thing that scared him the most was he didn't know if she would still pull the trigger when she did run out of chambers. He felt like that was something he should be confident about, especially when it came to his partner. But he wasn't.

And when he told her his fears? She hadn't listened.

Now, she was traipsing around abandoned houses and churches, chasing ghosts. It was just too much. Nora's life had been hard enough. She didn't need to make it harder. Jason just wished she could see that and understand where he was coming from. But she didn't. She always had something to prove, some fear to face, some excuse for putting her life on the line.

As much as he wanted to beg Nora to be different, it wasn't his place to do so. She was who she was, and he had to figure out how to be okay with it.

The thought exhausted him.

As she reached for the handle for the car door, he said, "I'm not going to apologize for caring, Nora."

"I never asked for you to," she snapped back.

Jason looked at her, sizing her up. She did the same.

"You get that I'm not trying to tell you how to live your life or whatever, right? I just want you to try and think for just a single millisecond before you jump into the ocean with a bunch of hungry Great White sharks swimming around. I don't think that's too much to ask," he sighed, hoping they could put this spat behind them.

"You're right. It's not too much to ask. I'll try to be more mindful and include you. I just didn't want to add more drama," she said.

In that moment, Jason could almost picture Nora as the fourteen year old girl who's life had been snatched from her so cruelly and left her to answer for it all just because she was the one who had escaped. It was like she was always trying to make up for the fact that she was the one who came home and not her sister.

"You're not adding more drama. You're my partner and my best friend. You are not a burden to me, and neither are your problems. Got it, Price?"

"Got it."

Jason had a feeling this wasn't the end of the argument, but he hoped it was settled for now. It was too charged a subject to fizzle so easily. Nora was the type of person who got angry when other people got angry with her. He knew it was a self-defense mechanism, but it drove him crazy. It also meant he was constantly having to watch his tone, stay calm, be the rational one, and sometimes, it was all just too much to keep up with.

For now, though, he hoped they were good.

"We're supposed to be meeting a Detective Matthew Wakefield with the Newell Sheriff's Office. I'm assuming the man smoking like a coal factory by the door is our guy," Jason said, pointing to the building across the street.

The man's suit was so wrinkled it looked like a pile of dogs had slept on it. His wavy hair was a little too long, like he hadn't been to a barber in months, and his eyes had deep, dark circles below them as if he hadn't actually been to bed in days.

"I'm taking it they don't have a lot of murders around here," Nora surmised as they both got out of the car.

Jason looked around. The faded crime scene tape haphazardly wound around the building was a pretty good indication this was not a normal Sunday evening in Newell.

Nora and Jason both pulled out their official identification and showed it as they approached the detective.

"Detective Wakefield?" Jason asked for confirmation.

The man dropped the cigarette and stepped on it before reaching out his hand to them.

"One and the same. Thanks for coming out. I've got to tell you I've never seen anything like this," he admitted.

"Just to clarify, is this where the first or second victim was found?" Jason asked. He could almost feel Nora roll her eyes at him. He'd never understand why it bugged her so much that he always tried to include the locals. She knew how territorial small-town police could get, and sugar was always going to get them more than salt.

"This is the second, Boyd Ewen. The first victim, Lynna McLean, was discovered at the old Trask Textiles building in Ellenton, Mass."

The detective motioned for them to follow him into the building.

"Watch your step. We've bagged and tagged everything, but it's still an OSHA violation just waiting to happen."

"Thanks," Jason nodded.

He looked over at Nora. She wasn't in her usual take-charge mode. Instead, she was looking all around the place with concern. She'd been digging through abandoned churches alone, and *now* she was concerned.

"You good?" he asked when he could not catch her eye.

"What? Yes. Just looking around, watching my step."

She gave him a confused look, like she wasn't sure why he was asking. Just as he was about to explain himself, she tripped over a raised mat and fell straight into him. He instinctively caught her, quickly helping her to her feet and letting her go. She loathed his knight in shining armor antics, so he always tried to play it off anytime he helped keep her upright when she started having one of her panic attacks or caught her when she almost fell.

"Guess I should pay better attention to where I'm going," she shrugged, her cheeks tinged with embarrassment.

"I see what he meant about the whole OSHA violation comment. Maybe next time you can catch me," he smiled, trying his best to bring some levity to the situation.

Nora gave him a slight smirk in return, which was more than he expected. Their job was hard enough, so he always tried his best to lighten the mood whenever he could.

They followed Detective Wakefield across the room, down some stairs and towards what Jason could only assume was the back of the building or a basement. As soon as the word *basement* came to mind, he drew his attention back to Nora.

She was tentatively following behind them, her pace slowing the darker their path ahead of them got. Jason noticed right away her shoulders were rolled inward protectively, like she was trying to make herself smaller.

She was falling into that mode. The mode she always fell into, when basements were concerned. He'd seen it before.

Nora could speak for herself, ask for help if she needed it. The problem was, she never did. Over the years, he'd figured out little ways he could step in, be helpful but not intrusive or suffocating.

"Hey, Detective? You got any lights in this place you can turn on? I can't see my hand in front of my face," Jason called out in front of him.

“The electricity to the building is off, but we got some work lights set up at the crime scene. It’s just a little further down this hallway,” the man explained.

Jason caught Nora’s attention and she nodded at him, as if to tell him she was fine. He knew she wasn’t, but she’d never admit it otherwise.

When they finally got to the murder scene, six sets of work lights lit the room up like daylight. Other than a few evidence markers, there wasn’t anything else to see.

“Is this it?” Nora asked as she came into the room.

“Pretty much. Other than the body and a stone spire, which is back at the precinct, there wasn’t much here.”

“Spire? Like from an archeological dig?” Jason asked.

The detective nodded and showed them a photograph. Jason stared at it.

“What the hell?” he breathed, and Nora nodded.

“That’s Lieutenant Fillmore. He’s getting some info from Keith Thayer, the security guy who found the body. Feel free to interrupt,” the detective said as he pointed out the two men across the room.

A young, uniformed police officer was talking with a balding, middle-aged man in black slacks and a grey polo shirt with a security logo on it. The older man seemed rattled, like he’d never seen a dead body before. Maybe he hadn’t.

Jason hesitated to see if Nora would take the lead. He knew it was important to her that others see her as equal or better, never weak. Sure enough, she marched in front of him and right over to the eyewitness.

"Hello, Mr. Thayer. I'm Nora Price, and this is my partner, Jason Snyder. We're agents with the FBI and would like to ask you a few questions. Is that okay?” she asked, her tone professional and firm.

“Sure, whatever you need. I’ve already been here all day,” the older man complained.

“Thank you, Mr. Thayer, for the information. We’ll follow up with you if we need to,” the uniformed officer said as he excused himself.

“Am I going to repeat everything I just told that guy to you two?”

“If you would not mind, but we’ll try to keep it short,” Nora nodded.

“Well, I do mind. I’ve been held up here all day and I have things to do!” he growled.

"I can imagine, and we appreciate your patience. We just want to make sure we capture every single thing you can remember, sir, because it could be the difference between a guilty and not guilty verdict," Nora said smoothly.

Jason looked at her. Maybe he'd been rubbing off on her. That was almost word-for-word something he would've said to the man. Actually, Jason was fairly certain he had said it to a witness before.

"Really? Me?" the man asked, his eyebrows reaching towards his receding hairline in surprise.

"Yes, sir. You could hold the key to blowing this whole thing wide open, and you don't even know it," she nodded.

Jason could not help but smile with pride. As much as Nora had teased him over the years for choosing to be charming rather than cutthroat, here she was charming the pants off this eyewitness. It felt good knowing she didn't think his methods were a complete waste of time, at least not enough to not use them herself when it suited her.

"Well, okay. If it'll help."

"Thank you, Mr. Thayer," Jason nodded.

The man explained he worked for a security company and had come to check out a tripped alarm at the auto shop when he found the body.

"I only got close enough to see the person wasn't breathing. Otherwise, I kept my distance until the cops got here. I've never seen anything like that before. Some of our buildings have been burgled, but nothing like this."

"Do you remember if all these work lights were here or if the police brought them in?" Jason asked.

"I'm not sure. It was early, and the place was dark except for this room. I had to use the flashlight on my phone."

"Did you notice anything else?" Nora asked.

"I don't think so. It was really awful," the man admitted as he looked down at his feet, almost like he was trying to hide his emotions, embarrassed by how much seeing a dead person affected him.

Jason started to say something, but Nora beat him to it.

"It sounds terrifying. I would not be nearly as calm as you are or be as much help to the authorities as you've been," she assured the man.

He looked up and gave her a slight smile, like he appreciated her effort but didn't quite believe her.

“Really, Mr. Thayer. Thank you for the extra time today. It’s been more helpful than you know,” Jason added.

The man nodded and asked if it was okay for him to leave. They both nodded in unison, understanding his need to get away from the dreadful scene.

Jason couldn’t agree more. He would’ve loved to leave, too. But he had a feeling they were only at the beginning of something big.

CHAPTER SIX

After finding all they could from the auto shop, which wasn't much, Nora and Jason pulled up to the foreboding, decaying Trask Textiles. The first victim had been found there two days before, a timeline that worried Nora. It was never good when there were just days between kills rather than weeks or months.

The building stood like a weathered monolith, a hulking mass of brick and stone towering over its surroundings. Windows, once lit with restless activity and endless fabric, now gaped like vacant eyes into the world outside as it moved on.

Lynna McLean had been found at the abandoned mill by a group of teenagers who had broken in to skateboard through the first floor. Now, a black and white sat out front, its high beams on facing the front of the building. The lights made the building look even more ominous as they approached.

The evening had given way to nightfall, and the slight chill of autumn hung in the air. Nora shivered as she stepped out of the car.

"Here," Jason said as he held out a black pullover with the FBI logo on the front.

"Thanks. Forgot to pack mine," she smirked. She didn't even know where her pullover was. But Jason was a perpetual Boy Scout. He was always prepared, always ready with a solution, or at the very least options. Nora wondered what that felt like – to never be caught with his pants down, figuratively speaking.

She slipped the pullover on and immediately felt relief from the biting wind. Jason caught her relishing the warmth and smiled wide, like he felt like he'd actually done something right. She smiled back, letting the ice wall she'd metaphorically put up between them begin to thaw.

"Hi there. Thanks for meeting us out here. This is Nora Price, and I'm Jason Snyder. We're agents with the FBI," Jason introduced as they walked up to the uniformed officer's car. They held out their credentials so he'd know they were who they said they were.

The uniformed officer stepped out of his vehicle and shook their hands. His grip was firm, but friendly. He had short, dark hair and light-colored eyes. There wasn't enough light around them for her to tell the exact colors of either.

"Hi, I'm Lieutenant Cecil Holbrook with the Ellenton Police Department. It's pitch black in that place, so I thought maybe my high beams would help," the officer said, doing his best to explain the strange setup.

"Where was the victim found?" Nora asked, dreading the idea of walking into the depths of a falling down textile mill.

"The body was found just inside the front entryway. Our crime scene technicians have already been through here and wiped the place clean, but I can escort you inside if you'd like."

"Yes, please. We won't stay long. The place doesn't look exactly... stable," Jason observed.

"You are correct, sir. This building has been condemned for over a year," the officer agreed.

Of course it was, Nora thought to herself.

Lieutenant Holbrook pulled a large, black tactical flashlight from his side and clicked it on as he led them towards the entrance of the building.

"Is there any debris we need to look out for?" Nora called to the officer. She already had to watch where she was going just from being naturally clumsy. She didn't want to have to worry about falling flat on her face or tripping over some errant piece of rubble, too.

"No, not at all," Lieutenant Holbrook said without missing a step.

The officer pulled the handle on the steel door and held it open for Nora and Jason. He knocked the kickstand down on the inside corner to keep the door from closing. Then, he shined his flashlight out in front of them.

A giant chamber of a room stretched out before them into the darkness.

Were old buildings like this like people? Haunted by what they used to be or the things they'd seen?

Nora easily imagined the place as a once bustling enterprise of clattering machinery and chatty workers as they went about their day.

Now, the building stood silent, echoes of the past long gone along with the inventory and people who had come before.

As the three of them ventured into the cavernous hall, an eerie stillness prevailed, broken only by the occasional groan of settling timbers. A mournful wind whispered through broken panes around them, making Nora grateful Jason had given her the pullover.

The scent of dampness and dead leaves permeated the air around them, but as she looked around the space, Nora didn't see remnants of leaves anywhere. A thick layer of dust coated the floor, except for where Lynna McLean had been found and the crime scene technicians had been.

"We left the markers in place so you could see where the body was and stuff, but otherwise, there isn't much to see," the officer said as he pointed to the crime scene.

"Gotcha. So the body was there?" Jason asked, confirming where exactly Lynna McLean had been found.

Nora immediately understood why Jason was asking for clarification. At this crime scene, there were three markers. At the second victim's crime scene, there'd only been two.

"Yes, the victim was there, a stone spire was there, and a kerosene lamp was there. Looked like she'd been hit over the head, strangled. Maybe dragged here, but there weren't any footprints in the dust."

"Was the lamp lit?" Nora asked, surprised at the variation between the two crime scenes.

"I believe so," the officer nodded. "Here's the photos we took."

Nora looked through them. Nora caught Jason's eye, and she could tell he was thinking the same thing. There wasn't any kind of lantern or lamp at the other crime scene. Just work lights. She made a mental note to ask again if there'd been some kind of light source at the auto shop when the witness found the body, or if the work lights had been set up by the crime scene techs.

"Did the crime scene techs take the stone spire back to the Ellenton Police Department or somewhere else?" Jason asked.

Good thinking, Nora thought. They needed to see if the two spires were the same. They certainly looked that way, from the photos.

"It was, but we officially transferred it to the Newell Sheriff's Office this afternoon. They have more resources than we do, and the detectives working the cases agreed it was better to keep them together," the officer said, raising his shoulders in a nonchalant shrug. He obviously had no dog in this fight.

Nora wondered if the Ellenton Police Department and Newell Sheriff's Office were friends or foes. It seemed to change from case-to-case, so she was never quite sure if the locals were cooperating with each other because they didn't want to embarrass themselves in front of the FBI, or they recognized it was better for the case to do so. Either way, Nora suspected the inconsistency was probably normal.

"All right. That means one less stop for us," Jason said matter-of-factly. Then, he added, "Thank you, Lieutenant Holbrook, for meeting us out here. We appreciate your time."

"No problem. And good luck," he said with a tight smile, almost like he wasn't sure what the right thing to say was.

"Thanks." Jason nodded.

*

"I hope they have some fresh coffee," Nora complained as they climbed the concrete stairs at the front of the Newell Sheriff's Office.

"Me, too," Jason agreed.

The Newell Sheriff's Office itself was a modest structure, housed in a turn-of-the-century brick building that had likely been repurposed from some other community-focused space.

Glass doors opened to a lobby with metal detectors, a large polished wooden counter, a row of lockers, and three uniformed police officers. One stood behind the counter while the other two manned the detectors.

Nora and Jason provided their credentials, signed in, and placed their weapons in assigned lockers. Then, one of the uniformed officers behind the counter escorted them down a narrow hallway to the right.

As they followed the officer, Nora noticed the walls were adorned with badges, plaques, and framed photographs, the familiar coziness of a small town seeping out of every nook and cranny. She imagined everyone knew everyone else, and strangers weren't strangers for long. Otherwise, they likely didn't stick around.

Nora wondered if the killer was already a part of their community, and if not, how did a stranger slip under the radar so easily? Maybe they lived on the outskirts of town, so they were a part of the community but not completely.

The uniformed officer led them to a large conference room in the back of the building. There, in the front of the room, were two stone spires. They weren't huge, maybe four feet tall, and reminded Nora of smaller versions of the Washington Monument or Vatican Obelisk. They had to have been heavy, too. They looked hand carved, smooth and unmarked, like someone took a lot of time designing and creating them out of a large slab of stone.

"Well, it makes sense the killer would choose abandoned buildings for their crime scenes. Could you imagine someone trying to drag these into a populated place? These things would've given them away in a heartbeat," Jason chuckled.

Thankfully, the uniformed officer had already left the room. Nora appreciated Jason's humor, but it wasn't for everybody, especially not when he was being salty or sarcastic.

"No kidding. What do you think they mean?" Nora asked.

"Maybe something political or religious?" he asked, his arched eyebrow emphasizing his curiosity.

"I didn't get that vibe from the locations we've been to, but we can't rule it out."

Nora could not recall a single case they'd worked that had been either political or religious in nature. In her experience, serial killers tended to have more singular tastes, other avenues they wanted to explore outside of town halls and churches. Although, the thought made her wonder about her own case.

If the man who kidnapped her and her sister had kept them in a church basement, did that have any bearing on the case? Or was it simply a means to an end, a place that happened to be available no one would look?

Nora's family wasn't particularly religious or political, so someone taking her and her sister for either of those reasons didn't make sense. Like most things, Nora could not remember the last time she'd gone to an actual church service. It was probably the Christmas before the abductions, but Nora didn't know.

After everything happened, her parents had retreated from any kind of social life they'd had before she and her sister had been taken. At the time, Nora had appreciated their choices, especially since she hated how people always stared at her expectantly, like they were waiting for her to have some grandiose epiphany that would solve everything and bring her sister home.

Now, Nora wasn't sure if self-isolation had been the best choice. What if that's what finally got to Trudie? As far as Nora knew, Trudie only spent her time at Wendy's Hope and the First Baptist Church. Maybe not expanding her social circle had only added more despair to her already sorrowful heart.

But now wasn't the time to be thinking about Trudie Whittier and her suicide. Still, she could not help it. She saw the parallels between her and Trudie, and even her mom and Trudie, and frankly, it scared her. Nora had been through a lot, but the one thing she knew without any doubt in her mind was she could not take any other kind of loss right now, or any time soon.

"Yeah. Maybe something about the victims will make it make sense, or perhaps their families will know something," Jason suggested, interrupting her thoughts.

"Hopefully. I think we should review the case files tonight, get our bearings, and then first thing tomorrow start the interviews. What do you think?" Nora proposed.

Jason looked at his phone, and she could tell by his baffled expression that he'd just realized how late it was.

"Agreed. But we definitely need to order some pizza or something because I'm starving," Jason complained.

Nora started to argue with him when her own stomach grumbled at her, effectively shutting her up.

"How do you always forget about food?" Jason asked, already knowing what she was going to say.

"Because I just get so wrapped up in my head...".

"You forget about your stomach. I know," he grumbled.

"Aww, you get me," she teased.

"Yeah, yeah," he said, wrinkling his nose at her.

Nora always loved when he did that. It was one of the few silly expressions she'd ever seen him make, and it always reminded her to not take herself so seriously. Sometimes, that was easier said than done.

She smiled and disappeared down the hallway, heading back towards the front of the building. Yes, Nora could look up somewhere to get food on her phone, but she thought it would be nice to get a recommendation from one or two people who ate locally all the time.

She approached the uniformed officers at the desk with a warm smile.

"Hi, gentlemen. My partner and I are in desperate need of sustenance. Any ideas on where we could order delivery from?" she asked, hoping she was coming across friendly and not flirty.

"Doyle's is a good spot. They're open all night, and they have free delivery. I think we have a menu. Just a second," one of the officers said. "Here's a menu. The sandwiches are great."

Nora returned to the conference room to find Jason had set up both of their laptops on the conference table at the back of the room. It was strange to have these two random stone spires just sitting at the front like they were about to give a speech or have a debate, but so far the case had kind of been strange.

"Apparently, there's a Club Sandwich and Turkey Reuben with our names on them at Doyle's Diner. And they deliver," she announced as she walked in.

"Sounds good to me. No mustard for me, please," he requested.

"No problem." Nora called the number on the menu and placed a delivery order. "Hey, do you want steak fries or chips?" she asked, holding the phone away from her mouth.

"If they're quick, fries. If not, chips," he answered.

"Did you hear that?" she asked the person on the phone.

Nora finished placing the order and gave them her pay card information. Then, she hung up the phone and sat down across from Jason.

"We still have a ton of work to do," Jason lamented, sounding stressed.

"Don't we always?" she asked, not expecting an answer.

So far, they'd visited the two crime scenes and seen the two stone spires, but they still didn't know much about their victims. They also hadn't gotten the chance to review the medical examiner's findings or any of the logged evidence. Nora was tired, but maybe ordering some food would give her a second wind.

One of the few things Nora did not like about being an FBI agent was how many all-nighters they had to pull. It was one thing if they were on a stakeout or something, where their adrenaline was elevated and something exciting could happen any minute. Reading page after page of evidence logs and autopsy notes made a long night even longer.

Nora's eyes started to cross just thinking about it. The food would help give them fuel for a little while, but she was pretty sure they were going to need something stronger.

“They said that the food will be here in ten minutes, so I’m going to put on another pot of coffee. I have a feeling it’s going to be an all-nighter,” Nora sighed, digging into the files on the victims.

CHAPTER SEVEN

Nora yawned and tried to concentrate on the questions she would need to ask the next-of-kin.

Libby Cates, Lynna McLean's older sister, was the first to arrive at the Newell Sheriff's Office. Her pale silver hair was pulled back into a loose chignon at the nape of her neck, her face etched with the lines of age and despair. Nora watched as she continuously dabbed at her red-rimmed eyes, swollen from crying, every movement sluggish from the weight of her grief.

"Thank you for coming in, Ms. Cates," Jason said as he held out the chair in the interview room for the woman. His tone was warm and encouraging, and most of all, genuine.

"This is a nightmare," the woman sniffled, touching the corners of her eyes again with a handkerchief with one hand as she clutched a worn beaded rosary in the other.

"We're so sorry for your loss," Nora added, but she knew as soon as the words left her mouth they didn't sound authentic.

The woman cut her eyes at Nora, something Nora hadn't expected. She decided it would probably be best if she took a backseat to Jason with this woman. Something about Nora did not seem to sit well with Libby Cates.

"Who could have done such a thing to my baby sister? She never did anything to anybody," the woman sobbed.

Nora hated dealing with the victims' loved ones. The open displays of emotion and untamed sorrow were foreign to her, and she didn't know how to deal with them.

Like everyone else who had experienced something horribly traumatic in their lives, Nora's life was divided into two categories: before the abduction and after the abduction. Before she and her sister had been taken, her family was jovial, outgoing, always people others seemed to want to have around. After the abduction, people crossed the street when they saw any member of Nora's family on the same side of the street. It was like people believed that they'd been touched by some inauspicious, unseen hand, and Nora's family carried some kind of plague of misfortune everywhere they went.

It wasn't true, but Nora had found people were naturally superstitious, and it was easier to believe it was something about their family that had attracted the trauma they'd gone through rather than the idea that sometimes bad people did bad things and no one knew why.

After the abduction, her family became quieter and more reserved, rarely expressing themselves within the walls of their own home, must less in public. The more time that passed after the incident, the more difficult it had become for Nora to be around emotional people. It made her extremely uncomfortable, especially when she was working a case.

"We're doing everything we can to find the person who took your sister from you. That's why it was important we talk to you about her today. Did Lynna have any enemies or anyone who might have been holding a grudge against her?" Jason asked, taking out his notepad to write down any clues the woman might provide.

"No. People loved Lynna. She was the best of us. She was the type of person who had given you her coat if you were cold, even if that meant she'd freeze to death. She even testified for that horrible man after he hurt her and all those people, just so they would not gas him," the woman hissed with more venom than a pit viper.

Nora and Jason looked at each other. What was she talking about?

"What man?" Nora asked, unwilling to wait for Jason to figure out a smoother way to ask Libby Cates the same question.

"Gary Barker. Last year, he robbed the bodega where Lynna was working. He killed three people and left Lynna in a coma for six weeks. We were sure we were going to lose her, too, but she pulled through. When she woke up, we all truly believed she'd survived because it just wasn't her time."

Libby Cates nervously rubbed her rosary, as if she was silently praying any minute they'd tell her Lynna was going to be okay, that she'd survived this horrible thing. Nora wished she could tell the woman that Lynna was going to wake up and come back to her, anything to make her feel better about her loss. But she could not.

Nora didn't know if Lynna had survived because it wasn't her time yet, or if she'd died because it was. That wasn't a question she had any idea how to answer. But she did know what it was like to not have her sister to go through life with anymore. There was nothing she could compare it to. And she also knew better than most that there was no reasoning with grief.

When Nora woke up in the hospital and heard Sophia wasn't home yet, she'd wanted to die. She'd wanted to close her eyes and never wake up again in a world where Sophia wasn't back home safe and sound with her family. No other existence made sense to her.

Then, she'd suddenly become the embodiment of hope, the one person who could bring Sophia home. But she could not. She could not tell the police or even parents anything because her mind was a blank canvas, almost as if the day she'd woken up in the hospital was her first day alive.

Before. After. Now, Libby Cates would have the same timeline to contend with, and Nora did not envy her.

"We all told her that man didn't deserve her forgiveness. But she didn't care. That's just who she was," the woman sniffled loudly, another wave of grief crashing over her.

"I remember that case. I remember the judge said it was only because of your sister that the defendant hadn't been sent straight to Death Row," Jason recalled.

Nora wondered if someone had targeted Nora because of her advocacy for Gary Barker's life. It was possible, but that didn't explain Boyd Ewen's death, unless they were somehow connected.

"Like I told her when she did it, careless people don't deserve to be cared for," the woman harrumphed as tears streamed down the sides of her face. Libby Cates clearly didn't agree with her sister's decision to defend the man who had almost killed her, but none of that mattered now. Her sister was gone. A victim of violence no one had seen coming. Again.

"Does the name Boyd Ewen ring any bells for you, Ms. Cates?" Nora asked, hoping to make some kind of connection with the second victim before Jason wrapped up the interview.

"No. Not at all. I'd remember a name like that. That poor man." The woman shook her head.

Nora struggled to keep a straight face. Libby Cates was quite the character. Nora could not help but wonder how she and her sister had gotten along, especially given how opinionated Libby seemed to be.

It was always hard for Nora to be around adult women who had sisters. They'd had the chance to grow up together, get to know each other in different ways, appreciate their differences. All Nora knew of her sister was mostly envy. Envy for how she looked, envy for how people treated her, and sometimes, even envy that she wasn't here to deal with how much of an impact her absence had made on their family and the community.

"You've given us a good place to start, Ms. Cates. Would it be okay for us to call if we have any more questions?" Jason asked. He always seemed to know not just when to wrap things up, but also the right way to do so.

"Yes, of course. And if you find out anything, you'll call then too, right?" she asked, worry in her voice.

"Absolutely," Nora reassured her.

The woman looked at Nora and then at Jason, who nodded. It was like she'd needed him to confirm Nora was telling the truth. Nora wondered if it said more about her or Ms. Cates that the woman needed more than Nora's word she'd call.

Probably me, Nora thought to herself.

Libby Cates thanked Nora and Jason for talking with her, although they hadn't said much and this hadn't been a social call. Then, she hesitated at the door, as if she wanted to say something else, but then continued forward without another word. Nora knew how hard it was to keep putting one foot in front of the other, especially when there weren't any answers, but she applauded the fact that Libby Cates did it.

"I'll get started on the Barker angle if you want to check and see if anyone's here for Boyd Ewen yet," Nora offered.

"Sounds good. I need to stretch my legs for a few anyways," Jason agreed.

So far, they hadn't found any overlap between Lynna McLean and Boyd Ewen. Lynna had been in her late twenties, she was single, and she still worked at a bodega. Nora wasn't sure if it was the same one where she'd been shot, but that was something she'd need to find out. Maybe one of the other victims' families or friends had held a grudge against Lynna for helping Gary Barker avoid lethal injection.

Lynna had spent most of her time working and doing prison advocacy work. Nora wondered if Libby Cates knew how many inmates her sister had helped. Probably not, she guessed based on how Libby spoke about her sister's advocacy work for Gary Barker.

She didn't have any pets, she'd never been married, and her social media history was limited to cat and comedy videos. She rented an apartment near the bodega where she worked, and she didn't own a car. She rode a bike around town or grabbed a rideshare on snow days. Overall, Lynna McLean lived a fairly simple life, so the fact that someone had murdered her made zero sense in the grand scheme of things.

The second victim, Boyd Ewen, was in his mid-fifties, and he'd been married for thirty-two years to the same woman. He had five children, thirteen grandchildren, and according to social media, two great grandkids (twins!) on the way. He was a retired Air Force colonel who had worked a few odd jobs here and there before he opened a successful forensic accounting firm in his late forties. The only legal cases he'd been involved with were related to fraud, corporate espionage, and hostile takeovers.

Boyd Ewen had been an avid golfer who appeared to only have joined various social media platforms to be able to see pictures of his kids and grandkids. He had no posts, no contact information, and no profile pictures. In fact, Boyd Ewen was still using an old dial-up email address even though he had one through his firm.

The two victims didn't appear to know each other. They didn't live in the same towns, go to the same churches, or even have any mutual friends by the looks of their social media accounts. Based on the case files and all the research Nora and Jason had done the night before, the victims were complete strangers.

Nora even expanded her search to see if anyone the victims knew were friends or relatives with each other, but nothing came up. They were two people just out there living their lives, running parallel to each other until they intersected with this killer, which appeared to be the only thing they had in common.

She knew from the Osmond Wright case that sometimes things weren't as simple as they seemed, and two opposite notions could be true at the same time. Nora wasn't sure if that was the case with Lynna McLean and Boyd Ewen, especially because they had zero overlap, but she had no doubt they were both killed by the same person.

Aside from the almost identical stone spires at both crime scenes, both victims had died from a combination of a blunt force trauma to the occipital region and strangulation. Even the indentions in the victims' skulls were the same, indicating the killer used the same weapon to knock them both unconscious.

The problem wasn't just the completely independent victimology. It was also the fact that nothing about the crimes indicated – or even hinted at – a motive. The crime scenes were too planned out to be random acts of violence that just happened to have the same cause of death. There was no indication either victim owed anyone money, and both victims still had all of their jewelry, money and credit cards on their person at the time of death. So, something financial didn't appear to be the motive.

There was no element of sexual violence, although Nora could argue the phallic nature of the stone spires was certainly something worth noting, although she had no idea how they tied into a motive. The only thing that made any kind of sense, given all the differences between the two victims and lack of any commonalities was some sort of vendetta.

She hoped the Gary Barker angle would give them something more to work with, but that seemed too easy. This killer was meticulous in their planning and execution. Nora didn't believe someone in prison who'd impulsively shot up a bodega the year before could've planned something like this. Plus, she felt like the stone spires symbolized something. She just had no idea what.

Nora sighed as she leaned back in her chair. She hoped whoever was coming to talk to them about Boyd Ewen would have some answers, or at least give them more of a place to start. So far, it just seemed like they were poking around in the dark, which meant that a killer was still on the loose and could strike at any moment.

CHAPTER EIGHT

It was getting close to midnight. Nora looked up from the table, where she'd been scouring the files until her vision blurred.

"This is Agent Nora Price. She's my partner," Jason said as he walked back into the room, a slight woman following quietly behind him.

The woman appeared to be around the same age as Boyd Ewen. She had a blunt cut salt-and-pepper bob, a sharp thin nose, and dark hazel eyes with dark, heavy brows furrowed above them.

"Hello," Nora said, sounding almost robotic.

"Hi," the woman nodded, her voice soft with sadness and loss.

"This is Martha Ewen, Boyd Ewen's wife," Jason introduced. He gestured to the chair for the woman to take a seat, but she just stood in place, like her feet were suddenly frozen to the floor.

Nora jumped to her feet and offered to guide the woman to the chair. Jason looked at her with an odd expression, like he wasn't sure what had just happened. Nora understood, though.

After Sophia had disappeared, she'd become completely immobile at the utterance of her sister's name. It was involuntary, but it was also consistent. It didn't matter where she was or what she was doing. If she heard Sophia's name, it was like she'd stuck her finger in a light socket and gotten electrocuted. It often felt that way, too.

Nora had thought for a long time that it was just this random thing that happened to her, like she was the only one who had ever experienced that kind of reaction. Then, on one of the first cases she'd worked with Jason, a man whose wife had been murdered had done the same thing. The moment she'd said his wife's name, he been stopped in his tracks. Nora had no idea what had happened, but she thought maybe something medically was wrong with the man, like he was having a stroke or something.

She'd quickly rushed to his side, desperate to make sure he was okay. As soon as she'd touched his arm, it was like the spell had been lifted. That was the moment Nora knew she wasn't the only one who'd been immobilized by grief.

The woman's eyes were downcast as she shuffled over to the seat, her footsteps heavy as though she were in a daze. She collapsed into the chair, breathing a sigh of relief, like she knew her legs could not hold her weight upright any longer.

"Would it be okay if I call you Martha?" Nora asked as she took a seat next to Mrs. Ewen. She didn't know if saying her last name would cause a freeze tag moment, or if it was just hearing her husband's first name that did it. Either way, Nora didn't want to find out.

"Yes, that would be fine," the woman nodded as she folded her arms tightly around her body. Nora's heart ached for the woman, knowing she was just doing her best to hold herself together.

"We are so sorry for your loss, Martha. We've been looking into your husband's affairs, and we were hoping you could shed some light on anyone who might have wanted to do him or your family harm," Nora explained. She knew she didn't sound as slick as Jason, but she was trying. That had to mean something, right?

"Oh, I absolutely know who you should be looking into. Leon Prescott. My husband was the forensic accountant in his embezzlement case. He was found guilty on all counts," Martha Ewen stated, her tone resolute and bitter.

"Did Leon Prescott say or do anything that makes you think he's the culprit?" Jason asked curiously.

"He threatened Boyd. When the jury found him guilty, that man looked right at my husband and in front of God, the judge, and the jury told him he was going to 'end him'," the woman declared, using air quotes around the last two words for emphasis.

"Do you recall when that was?" Jason asked, taking notes.

"Six months ago. Since then, my Boyd was taking some time to decide what he wanted to do next. The stress was really getting to him, and we wanted to focus on our family. If you ask me, I think he was worried Leon Prescott would make good on his threat."

Martha Ewen suddenly hunched over and tightly covered her mouth. Nora started to ask her what was wrong when the woman being to shake, her body wracked with muffled sobs. Nora looked at Jason, unsure if she should try to comfort the woman or just let her be.

Nora decided it was best to give the woman time. She'd just lost her husband, a man she'd been with more than half her life. It made sense she'd be wracked with uncontrollable emotions. It had always made sense, but it had never made Nora any less uncomfortable.

After the abductions, Nora's mother had what she'd called "spells". She'd tell Nora and her father that she felt a "spell" coming on and she had to go lie down. Nora had thought it was strange, but then she just figured her mom needed time alone.

One time, about six months after Sophia's memorial, Nora had checked in on her mother after one of her "spells". She found her face down on her bed, uncontrollably sobbing into a pillow. It had broken Nora's heart to see her mother so grief-stricken, but even more so to know her mother felt like she had to hide that away from her and her dad.

Nora wondered if her mother had been more extroverted with her grief if she'd still be so uncomfortable when others got hysterical over the loss of their loved ones. It was hard to say. It wasn't the experience she'd had.

"Martha, would you like me to get you some water?" Jason asked, his need to problem-solve kicking in.

"Yes... ice cold... please," the woman managed through strained whimpers.

Jason hurried out of the room like it was a house on fire. Nora wished she'd thought of offering the woman something to drink. It would've given her a chance to get away from all the crying and tears.

Nora knew it wasn't typical to be as stoic as she was. Her mother had even pointed out how she'd never cried growing up, not even over sappy commercials or movies. She'd just sat there, taking it all in but never reacting. She'd never learned how to exert herself emotionally, and at this point she didn't want to. Some days, her grief swallowed her like a tsunami wave of pain. Those days were the hardest. Everything became muted – colors, sounds, feelings. Other days, it could be a puddle she stepped in, barely there, an annoyance that interrupted her good time. Most days, though, were fell somewhere in between.

Jason returned with a paper cup, ice cubes clinking inside of it, and placed it in front of the woman.

"Here you go, Martha," he said softly and then sat down.

"I'm sorry. I'm just... I'm a mess. I don't even know... I'm not sure what I'm supposed to do now. Boyd... he handled everything. Even my kids are at a loss," Martha sobbed.

Nora felt so badly for the woman. She'd felt awful for Libby Cates, too, but Libby's whole life didn't seem to be as intricately wrapped up in her sister as Martha's life was intertwined with her husband.

Loss was loss, but something about Martha Ewen's devastation felt more severe. Maybe it was just because Nora knew what it was like to lose her sister. She had no idea what it would be like to lose the love of her life after decades together. Even the thought of it made her stomach turn.

"Martha, is there someone we can call for you? One of your children maybe?" Nora proposed. She knew the woman wasn't going to be able to answer any more questions, and she certainly could not drive in the state she was in.

"My son... he dropped me off," she sniffled.

"I'd be happy to call him for you if you'd like," Jason offered.

Nora rolled her eyes at him when Martha wasn't looking. He was taking every opportunity to get away from the weeping woman. She didn't blame him, but she also didn't like being left to comfort her, especially when he knew she wasn't any good at it.

"Okay... he's the last number I called."

Martha unlocked her phone and handed it over to Jason.

"Before you go, Martha, may I ask you one other thing?" Nora requested.

Martha nodded in agreement but didn't say anything out loud. Nora suspected it was because she didn't trust her voice to remain steady.

"Did you or your husband know someone named Gary Barker?" Nora asked, hoping Martha could help her make a connection between Lynna McLean and Boyd Ewen.

"The guy that shot up that bodega last year? No. Boyd didn't work with criminals like *that*," she snapped.

"I'm sorry. I didn't mean to imply..." Nora said as she gave Martha Ewen a tight smile and nodded in understanding. She hadn't meant to insult her or her husband's memory. She'd just been hoping to figure out how the killer had picked their victims.

"No, I'm sorry. I just... I don't know why anyone would do this, but if I had to start somewhere, I'd start with Leon Prescott."

"Then, that's what we'll do," Nora promised.

They were missing a detail, but she had no clue what it could be. It seemed like there was some connection between these two victims. There had to be, or else the killer was just picking off people at random, and that was unlikely. There had to be something. They just needed to keep digging.

*

"Anything?" Nora asked as she let out a long, frustrated sigh.

"Not yet," Jason shook his head and yawned. "I think we should call it a night."

They'd been combing through every possible connection they could make between Lynna McLean and Boyd Ewen. So far, they hadn't found any links between the victims at all, not even a blood type.

Jason had looked further into Gary Barker, but he was living in solitary confinement upstate. According to the prison records, no one visited him or wrote him, and he only spoke with his lawyer once a month for updates on his appeals. Both of his parents were deceased, and he didn't have any other kin on file.

Nora was still waiting on the evidence files from Leon Prescott's trial, but so far, she hadn't found anything that tied him to Lynna McLean.

"I was thinking we should give Libby Cates a call. She seemed to be really close to her sister, so she might know if Leon Prescott had ever crossed Lynna's path. What do you think?" Nora asked, frustrated she hadn't found some kind of thread to pull on and unravel this mystery.

"I'm all for it if you think it'll help," Jason said as he scrolled through a document on his computer.

"I do, but I think you should call her," Nora said, fully serious.

Jason stopped tapping his keyboard and looked up at her.

"Excuse me, what did you say?"

"*You* should, you charmer, you. She liked you, trusted you. I think she'll respond better to you than she would to me," Nora explained.

"Fine. What's the number?" he said.

Nora tore off the corner of the yellow notepad she was scribbling notes on, wrote down Libby Cates' number, and slid it across the table to Jason.

He sighed and shook his head like he could not believe she was making him call the woman.

"You could have said no," Nora defended, arguing with his reaction.

"I feel like you would argue with a wall if you decided it looked at you wrong," he shook his head.

Nora gave him a dirty look, although she knew he was probably right.

"Hi, Ms. Cates? This is Jason Snyder, one of the FBI agents you spoke with earlier. Do you have a quick minute? Unfortunately, no I don't have any news at the moment, but we did come across something and I wanted to ask you about it," he said into the phone.

Nora admired how easy it was for Jason to talk to strangers. It seemed as easy for him as breathing. Nora wondered what that was like, always knowing what to say, how to say it, and when to say it. The only time she knew for sure it would come in handy to be more like Jason was when people had overstayed their welcome.

It didn't matter if it was overnight guests, dinner guests, or just someone stopping by her desk to say hi. She didn't know how to politely usher them along. Instead, she'd just ask people to go, leave, finish up, and it had never gone well no matter how many chances she got to try a different tactic.

She had no doubt her abduction had crippled any extroversion she may have had, but she also could not remember it ever being easy for her to talk to people she didn't know – even when she was little. For Sophia, no one had been a stranger, and that's also how the world saw her – the girl everyone loved, everyone wanted to know, and everyone wanted to call their friend.

Sometimes the hardest thing about Sophia's disappearance was the fact that Nora believed, without any doubt in her mind, that Sophia would do life way better than she ever had. She would've been popular – she already was, she would've had boyfriends, she would've probably cured cancer or some other terrible affliction. Nora imagined Sophia would've already been married with kids, spending weekends with their parents, the house so full of joy and light. Just like Sophia.

Nora shook all the ways she was a failure in comparison to her sister from her mind and refocused on Jason's conversation with Libby Cates.

"During our research, Ms. Cates, we came across a gentleman's name, and we were trying to figure out if Lynna might have known him. Well, he could have been someone she even knew a long time ago, so who better to ask than you?" Jason asked, his flattery clearly working.

Nora shook her head. This was exactly why he was on the phone with Ms. Cates, and she wasn't. The woman probably would've hung up on her by now.

"Yes, his name is Leon Prescott. Does that ring any bells? Oh, okay. I can hold." He covered the mouthpiece and said to Nora, "She needed to let her dog in from outside."

Nora nodded in understanding.

"Yes, I'm still here. Yes. Leon Prescott is his name. It does? How so? Really? For how long? Ah. Okay. Yes, you've been a great help. No, nothing else for now. We'll call when we know more. I promise. Okay, thank you, Ms. Cates. Goodbye," he said as he tapped the phone to end the call.

"Well?" Nora asked, eager to hear whatever Ms. Cates had said.

"Apparently, Lynna and Leon used to date before he got tied up in all of his legal troubles."

"They dated?" Nora asked, her eyes wide.

How did we miss this?

"Ms. Cates said it hadn't been anything too serious, but Lynna had broken it off when Leon got arrested."

"Well, maybe it was serious to *him*," Nora said pointedly.

"Maybe. Or maybe she knew something about his business dealings. Either way, we've finally got our connection." Jason grinned proudly.

"Yeah... so, are we thinking then that this was somehow related to the fraud charges? Because I thought Martha Ewen said he'd been acquitted," Nora said aloud more to herself than to Jason.

"No, she said he'd been found guilty on all counts," Jason corrected.

"Ah, okay. Then, that could be a motive, I guess." Nora shrugged.

"Could be. Besides, if he had been acquitted, it wouldn't necessarily mean he was innocent. Just that the jury couldn't convict beyond a reasonable doubt."

No truer words had ever been said.

Nora checked her watch. It was after one. She didn't want to waste the time with sleep, but Jason looked dead on his feet. Her fingers itched to dig more. This new connection was definitely something worth looking into.

CHAPTER NINE

The man stared at the different types of kerosene lamps, trying to decide which ones he liked best. The work lights he'd left at the auto shop had been cumbersome to set up, and they didn't give him the same ambient glow as the early morning or late afternoon sunlight would. The kerosene lamp at the textile mill had worked well, creating a long, pointed shadow from the obelisk just like he wanted.

There were so many different kinds of lamps and lanterns to choose from. The one he'd left at Trask Textiles was more of a camping-style kerosene lantern. It seemed like the safest and least expensive option so far, but it still wasn't quite what he wanted.

The man had looked online to see what he could find. He preferred the privacy of shopping on the internet, and he also liked how abundant the choices and inventory were. He'd found some knock-off vintage glass kerosene lanterns on a discount website, but then canceled his purchase when he realized he'd have to give his real identity and shipping information.

He didn't want to get caught because he'd left an obvious digital fingerprint that would lead the authorities back to him.

When he'd gotten off work earlier in the day, he'd driven for more than two hours until he found a big box hardware store a few towns over. He'd be one of hundreds of customers, which provided him at least a little anonymity. He'd worn dark colors, donned a ballcap, and kept his head down as he walked in, knowing there were cameras on the door watching him. His body might be captured on film, but there would not be anything identifiable about him if he could help it.

It was important he buy the right kind of light source for his work. The work lamps had been far too bright for what he wanted, and he needed something more self-sustaining like a lantern. He liked the old-fashioned feel of the kerosene lamps, but he also wasn't a fan of fire, especially because it could burn out. If it got knocked over somehow, it could ruin his whole plan.

In front of him, there were four different styles of lamps to choose from. There was a kerosene camping lantern like he'd left at Trask Textiles. There was an all-glass lamp, but it looked too fragile. There was a lamp with a metal bowl for holding the kerosene with an ornate glass hood.

The last one looked like it might be the right fit. It was mostly metal with a glass-like material around the bulb, and it appeared to be battery-operated. He checked out the display model to see if it had different lighting levels and was surprised to find it did. The sign next to the model also said the batteries were included, making the decision easy for the man to pick this one.

He pulled every boxed lamp from the shelf – four in total – and put them in his shopping cart. He wasn't sure how many he needed, but he figured this was a good start. The man hoped he could use a self-checkout option, especially because he knew how important it was to keep his interactions with other people to a minimum. The last thing he wanted was some old man at a home goods style store turning him into the cops.

He headed towards the front of the store.

When he got to the checkout stations, he was happy to find they did have a self-checkout lane open. He hurried through the checkout process and guided the shopping cart out to his vehicle. Once he placed his purchases in the back of his vehicle, he wiped the cart down with extra-strength bleach disinfecting wipes he'd gotten from work.

The drive back to Newell gave the man time to think. He felt good about the lanterns he'd picked out, that they would help deliver his message more clearly than anything else could. So far, nothing he'd read in the papers or online had captured his intentions the way he'd hoped.

People needed to understand they could not steal from others without there being consequences. There was a natural order to things, and he could not let anyone else take what didn't belong to them. Maybe they didn't see or understand the message, but soon it would all make sense. It was just a matter of time.

He didn't know if Aline would've approved of his methods, but he felt like she'd agree with his reasoning. Thieves had to be punished, and if no one else was going to stop them, he had to do it.

As far as he was concerned, he didn't have a choice.

CHAPTER TEN

Nora and Jason spent the following morning combing through Boyd Ewen's forensic accounting records, reading everything they could about Leon Prescott. He'd been found guilty on the embezzlement charges, but the case was under appeal. There was still a lot of evidence indicating Leon Prescott had committed several other types of fraud, but now with Boyd Ewen out of the picture, Nora wasn't sure what would happen.

"What happens if his appeal is granted?" Nora asked Jason.

"What do you mean?"

"Boyd Ewen was a key witness in the trial. He can't testify from beyond the grave," Nora scoffed.

"Well, he sort of can. It just depends on the judge," Jason countered.

"What do you mean?" she asked, confused.

"They'll have to file motions and stuff, but if the judge deems Boyd Ewen's testimony from the original trial admissible, then technically it's like Boyd Ewen is testifying from beyond the grave," Jason smiled.

"But what about Leon Prescott's right to cross-examine his accusers or whatever?" Nora challenged.

"Well, unless they prove Boyd Ewen's testimony is bias or something, he was already cross-examined and that would be the testimony on record for the new trial. But there are a lot of ways Leon Prescott's lawyers could get around that," Jason explained.

"I'm glad you were pre-law. It makes my life so much easier," Nora smiled at him.

"No problem, Price. Just call me your one-stop lawyer shop," he laughed, which made Nora laugh, too.

Leon Prescott was the owner and CEO of Prescott Holdings, Inc, which appeared to be an umbrella corporation for a number of smaller businesses. All of the businesses operated out of a strip mall, which also had Leon Prescott listed as the owner. There was a nail salon, a barber shop, a payday loan place, a mail shop, and a mom-and-pop tax preparation service.

Boyd Ewen had supposedly uncovered proof of potential insurance fraud after the nail salon had a fire, counterfeiting at the mail shop with fake stamps, and identity theft from the tax preparation place. In fact, based on Boyd Ewen's notes, Leon Prescott's hands were in every single pot of stolen money, all of which he'd failed to report on his taxes – another crime in and of itself.

"According to Boyd Ewen, Leon Prescott is a criminal mastermind. A very *wealthy* criminal mastermind," Jason commented.

"And?" Nora asked, sensing there was something he wasn't saying.

"Apparently, no one can find the money." He shrugged.

"What do you mean?" Nora asked, confused.

"Look, I'm surprised he didn't get off on the embezzlement charges because they did not prove Leon Prescott had ever had more money than what he reported. No offshore accounts, no secret safes in his home, nothing. If he's hoarding all this cash, where's he keeping it?" Jason wondered aloud.

"Maybe he's just that good at cooking the books," Nora suggested.

"Maybe. Or maybe that's why he killed Lynna and Boyd. They figured out where the money was."

"I think we're speculating entirely too much," Nora pointed out.

"Yeah, but that's all we have is speculation. Boyd never found solid, irrefutable proof of anything he believed Leon Prescott was guilty of doing. He even wrote himself a note that just says 'Proof' with a question mark," Jason sighed.

"Then, I think it's time we go talk to Leon Prescott himself and get his side of the story," Nora said matter-of-factly.

"I agree. I also think we need to grab something to eat on our way. I can't interrogate a suspect on an empty stomach," he joked.

Nora rolled her eyes. Of course, Jason was thinking about food. She never had to worry about going hungry because his stomach went off like an alarm clock at every mealtime.

"Fine, but it's going to be fast food and it has to be on the way," Nora bargained.

They picked up some burritos from a local drive-thru restaurant that served every kind of fast food there was – pizza, burgers, tacos, you name it. The burritos seemed the easiest and most filling.

"Do you think it's possible that Lynna and Boyd knew where the money was, and that's why he killed them?" Jason asked as he took a sip from his soft drink, his eyes never leaving the road.

"I don't know. His relationship with Lynna McLean is tenuous at best, and we don't have anything concrete tying him to either murder. I think we'll know more once we hear what he has to say," Nora said as she finished up the last bite of her bean burrito.

They hadn't found much else on Leon Prescott besides his legal troubles. He was in his late fifties, had never been married, and had no children. He occasionally played golf, sometimes with Boyd Ewen, but otherwise all he did was work.

He'd never lived anywhere but Newell, and he didn't even have a passport – this was an important part of his defense when prosecutors said he'd likely deposited the embezzled funds in an offshore account in the Cayman Islands or somewhere similar. He'd never had the means to leave the country, so therefore he could not have secret stacks of cash around the globe. Or at least that's what his defense team wanted the judge and jury to believe.

Nora and Jason had laughed about the defense's reasoning the first time they'd read it. People with means knew how to get around the law, and if Leon Prescott did have money tucked away, that's likely what he'd done. Besides, who's to say he'd traveled under his own name?

Regardless of what anyone thought, Leon Prescott's lawyers had been convincing enough to ensure he was found not guilty on all charges. He still had the risk of new charges being brought, but now double jeopardy applied for all the old stuff.

But what could Boyd Ewen and Lynna McLean have known about Leon Prescott to make him murder them? Even if they knew where he'd hidden his money, it wasn't like he could be charged for embezzlement again, not after he'd been acquitted.

If Leon Prescott was the killer, it would have to have to do with a lot more than just money. Lynna McLean and Boyd Ewen had both been killed in a personal way, suggesting the killer either knew them personally, had something against them, or both.

This was the only thread they'd found so far that connected the murders outside of the M.O. used. Nora hoped by pulling on this thread, they'd solve the case and call it a day. In an ideal world, that's exactly what would happen. Hope would win out, they'd catch the killer, and any potential victims this killer had planned on murdering would be safe.

Nora knew hope was dangerous, but sometimes it was all she had to get her through her day.

Leon Prescott's house was modest and no indication that he was or ever had been a man of means. It was a square, symmetrical home with a gabled roof and simple front porch area with an overhang. The earthy tones of the brick blended seamlessly into the natural landscaping around it, making it feel like it was embedded in nature rather than sitting on top of it.

Nora didn't see a doorbell, so she knocked loudly on the door. Jason stood off to the side, sizing up the surroundings. He was always on alert, always ready to defend and protect.

She heard a shuffling sound and a couple of clicks before the door opened. An older balding man with thick, black horn-rimmed glasses stared back at them.

"Yes?" he croaked at them.

"Mr. Leon Prescott?" Nora asked, wanting the man to confirm he was the person they needed to talk to.

"Go on and show your credentials," he said dismissively.

Nora and Jason pulled out their badges and displayed them for Mr. Prescott. He barely glanced at them before he gestured for them to follow him inside. Nora tentatively stepped into Leon Prescott's home, the aged wood floors creaking beneath her.

"Have a seat wherever. You thirsty?" the man asked gruffly.

"No, thank you," Nora declined politely. Jason silently shook his head when Leon Prescott looked at him.

Nora and Jason sat down on an old, frayed grey sectional while Leon Prescott sat across from them in a brown, cracked leather recliner. Everything in the home looked almost as old as Leon Prescott, with some things looking even older. There was an odd odor wafting through the space, a mixture of stale food and dirty laundry. Whatever it was, it stank.

"So, why are two agents from the Federal Bureau of Investigation in my house and sitting on my couch?" Leon Prescott asked with a sneer. He didn't seem concerned by their presence at all. His tone held an air of arrogance, like he somehow knew they could not possibly be there because of something he'd done.

"We'd like to talk with you about Boyd Ewen," Jason said, pulling out his trusty notepad and pen from his jacket pocket.

Leon Prescott mimicked a spitting gesture at the sound of the victim's name.

"Do not say that name in my presence," he scoffed.

"Unfortunately, Mr. Prescott, we're going to have to say Mr. Ewen's name. We're investigating his murder," Nora reproached the old man.

"I'm sorry, what did you just say?" Leon Prescott asked, taken aback. He looked genuinely shocked at the words that had just come out of Nora's mouth.

"Boyd Ewen was murdered," Jason reiterated, with less charm than usual.

The old man grabbed his chest in disbelief.

"What has this world come to?" the man suddenly wailed. His entire demeanor disintegrated into uncontrollable sobs and sadness, like Boyd Ewen had been immediate family or a close, personal friend. Nora wasn't buying it.

"We know this must be difficult for you, but we're speaking with everyone who knew Mr. Ewen. His wife, Martha, indicated there was most certainly a history between you two," Nora said, ignoring the man's sorrow. It felt performative and inauthentic the way he was going on.

Leon Prescott struggled to pull himself together. The more his body was wracked by the onslaught of grief, Nora began to doubt her initial assessment. Maybe this man was genuinely stricken by the loss of Boyd Ewen.

Nora looked at Jason, who shrugged back at her, like he wasn't sure if the man was being serious or just putting on a show.

"Forgive me... I just... not Boyd," the man sobbed. Then, he added, "Who would do such a thing?"

"Mr. Prescott, we need to know where you were Friday morning," Jason asked, hoping the redirection would give the man a chance to calm down.

"What?" Leon Prescott sniffled as he wiped his eyes, still unable to fully regain his composure.

"Actually, we need to know where you were early Friday morning and yesterday morning," Nora corrected. They might as well get his alibi for *both* murders while they were there.

"Why?" the man asked, his eyes alight with scrutiny.

"So far, Mr. Prescott, you haven't answered any of our questions. Would it be easier to talk at the Newell Sheriff's Office?" Jason challenged.

The man seemed to sober up at the sharpness of Jason's tone.

"I was at my office. Both days. Every day. I start at five a.m. and don't come home until six or seven at night," he replied hastily, almost like he wanted to reassure them he was being cooperative.

"Which office?"

"I have a suite of offices above the shops in town. Honestly, what is this all about?"

Nora cringed. Her dad used to always tell her and Sophia when they were kids that anyone who started a sentence with *Honestly* or *Trust me* was usually someone about to tell you a lie.

"In addition to Boyd Ewen's death, we're also investigating Lynna McLean's untimely demise," Nora answered, growing more irritable by the minute.

"Who?"

"Mr. Prescott, we know you know Lynna McLean. Her sister, Libby, said you two were dating when you were first arrested," Jason stated, his tone unusually acidic.

"Oh, good grief, that was ages ago. I don't even remember who I had lunch with last week, let alone who I might've took out to dinner who knows how long ago," he huffed.

"We'll need the name of any witnesses who can corroborate your whereabouts on Friday and yesterday," Nora pressed.

"My secretary, Dana Bridges, can confirm I was at the office all day. So can my lawyer, Mitchell Rutherford. I have standing appointments with him at the beginning and ending of every week," he said, possibly the first honest thing to come out of his mouth.

Nora's heart sank. A part of her knew Leon Prescott wasn't their man, but she'd still hoped he was so they could wrap this case up and go home. She also knew she'd rather keep investigating until she found the right bad guy than just put any bad guy away for something they actually didn't do.

Nora knew sometimes the easiest thing wasn't the right thing, but it didn't mean she didn't still want things to be easy. Something about this case bugged her, got under her skin more than any of the other cases they'd had. She wasn't sure why, but it was still there, gnawing at her like a dog with a bone.

"Write down their names and contact numbers for me, please, Mr. Prescott, and we'll be in touch," Jason said as he stood up and handed the man the notebook and pen to scribe the requested information.

Nora stood up with him, more than ready to get out of the stuffy time capsule Leon Prescott called home. They had another lead to follow.

CHAPTER ELEVEN

"What was that smell?" Nora asked once they were safely inside the vehicle and headed back to the Newell Sheriff's Office.

"I don't know, but it was awful," Jason declared, laughing the whole time.

"It was like a combo of sweaty gym socks and rotten tomatoes. Do you think he's just used to it or something?" Nora wondered aloud, unsure how anyone could ever get used to such a putrid smell.

"Probably, but it's more likely his olfactory senses are severely impaired," Jason surmised.

"*Severely* is an understatement," she giggled.

Even when things were difficult and they didn't have any leads, Nora was grateful they could still find something humorous to chuckle about. It might not have been appropriate to poke fun at Leon Prescott's bog of unending stench, but it sure as heck was funny.

The drive across town was peppered with red light after red light. It should have been a ten-minute drive at most, but instead, they kept having to stop every forty-five seconds.

"I think we need to see what we can dig up on those obelisks," Nora suggested as Jason pulled up in front of the sheriff's station.

"I didn't find anything in my initial search, but my search wasn't really focused on them."

"Same," Nora agreed.

Once Nora and Jason got their computers up and running, they both leaned against the conference room table, staring at the obelisks.

"Well?" Nora asked, not sure what they should do next.

"Let's do it," Jason said, doing his best to get them riled up.

Nora and Jason circled the two stone obelisks like tigers hunting their prey, sizing them up at every turn. Nora crouched down next to one of them, closely examining every inch of the surface she could see. She was determined to figure out where they came from and what they meant.

Nora had no idea if the shape or material was supposed to mean something, or if the object itself was serving another purpose. The only obelisks Nora knew about were famous monuments like the one in Washington. She'd discovered there were many others around the world, but still nothing about them seemed to offer any insights about the killer or why they were murdering people.

Based on everything Nora had read so far, obelisks were meant to commemorate the dead. They were reverential, and they typically honored figureheads or religious deities. None of that made sense when she tried to connect it back to the victims. Boyd Ewen and Lynna McLean were just regular people. They worked, they lived their lives, and she hadn't found anything that made them stand out in a way that would be worth honoring with something like a stone spire.

She studied the stone, fairly certain it was granite.

Did the composition of the obelisk mean anything? Was there something symbolic about granite?

These questions and more bounced around Nora's brain. Nothing was adding up, which was only making her more and more frustrated.

"Anything?" Jason asked, his tone clear he was coming up empty-handed.

"I'm not sure yet," Nora shrugged. Then, she added, "Grab me a pair of gloves, would you?"

Jason retrieved two sets of blue latex gloves from a box in his messenger bag, prompting Nora to give him an inquisitive look.

"What? It keeps them sterile if I keep them in the box," he explained as he handed a set to her.

"So you took a whole box?" she asked, incredulous.

"It's not like we won't use them, Nora," he rolled his eyes.

Nora pulled each glove on and then returned to inspecting the obelisk. The stone was smooth, and the shape was carved out of a single piece of what appeared to be granite.

There were no markings on any of the sides or the top of the spire, so she decided to look at the bottom. It was heavier than she expected, which made her feel like it was even more important she see what was underneath.

"Can you please help me lift this? I'm trying to see if there's anything on the bottom here," she asked.

Jason helped to gently guide the obelisk on its side so Nora could get a better look. At first, it looked like the bottom of the spire was rough-cut stone with nothing else to help identify where it had come from. Then, Nora noticed the roughness had ridges to it, like there was something else carved there.

"Can we lay it down on the floor? I think there's something carved here, but I can't tell with the lighting," she said.

Jason helped her guide the spire to the floor carefully. Nora pulled out her phone and turned on the flashlight app to see if more light would help her. There, in the middle of the base of the obelisk was a rough carving of an evil eye symbol with an "O" and an "L" carved on each side of it.

*

"Do you think whoever made those spires is local?" Jason asked, looking up from his laptop. They'd both been trying to track down any information they could online about who could have made the obelisks and where they'd come from. So far, they'd found nothing.

"Maybe. What search terms have you tried?" Nora asked, wondering what they were missing.

"Stone. Obelisk. Evil eye. I'm kind of drawing a blank, to be honest," Jason sighed.

"I looked up stone sculptures and stone carvers, but so far I haven't found any matches either," she lamented, shaking her head at their lack of progress.

Nora tried a few more search terms. When nothing yielded the results she wanted, she groaned with frustration.

"You okay?" Jason asked, surprised by her feral outburst.

"I feel like we keep running headfirst into brick walls. It's honestly the one part of this job I could do without, and it feels like this case has a lot more brick walls than any of our other cases combined," she admitted.

Nora had always liked puzzles and solving problems. But after everything that had happened and she couldn't remember anything that helped find Sophia, everything changed. She'd become tenacious about finding answers, determined beyond reason to make the connections that would lead her to solutions.

Lately, though, it had seemed like it was getting harder and harder to connect the dots. She didn't know if criminals were getting more sophisticated or if she was just losing her edge. Something felt off, though, and she wasn't sure what it was.

It could be her obsession with finding her abductor – and hopefully her sister. It could be her sheer exhaustion from the night terrors that seemed to plague her at every turn. There was always something getting in her way – the gaping hole in her memories, lack of information, encoded messages, the list went on and on. But none of these were anything new.

Nora wanted to solve this case, just like she'd wanted to solve all the other cases she'd worked. She wanted to find the person who had killed Boyd Ewen and Lynna McLean and make sure they didn't kill anyone else. The anxiety produced by the possibility of their finding another victim drove her forward. She had to keep looking. Something would turn up – it always did – as long as they both kept searching.

"I might have found something," Jason announced.

Nora perked up. "What?"

"There's a retired mason who lives about an hour away named Orman Lamprou," he said, summarizing something he was reading on his computer.

"The initials. O. L. That could be him," Nora said, a jolt of delight running through her veins. This possible lead couldn't have come at a better time.

"It looks like he does all kinds of stonework. He's in Abbottsville, which is about an hour away."

"Let's go," Nora said, quickly getting up from her chair and grabbing her FBI jacket.

CHAPTER TWELVE

Jason pulled into a parking spot directly in front of Stone and Bloom, the garden décor shop owned by Orman Lamprou.

The shop's exterior was a blend of rustic and whimsical touches, with stone garden gnomes on each side of the door. Other stone sculptures sat along the front of the shop – a rabbit sitting up on its hind legs, a cat keeping a watchful eye with a curious tail weaving into the air, a small gargoyle perching with outstretched wings, and more. The carving was crisp, the statues lifelike.

A weathered wooden sign hung above the door, it's lettering a vibrant and welcoming green. Antique bird cages of various sizes and colors were suspended with wire from the eaves, each overflowing with climbing vines and blooming flowers. The rigidness of the stone statues were softened by the abundant plant life.

Nora pushed open the glass door, eliciting a soft chime from somewhere above them as they stepped inside. Plants of all shapes and sizes adorned the large, open area that stretched out before Nora and Jason. Stone sculptures were strategically placed in the rows between the plants so they could not be overlooked.

"Welcome to Stone and Bloom! Be right with you," a man called out to them from somewhere in the back of the room. His tone was hurried yet inviting. Nora wondered if he was who they were looking for.

"Hey, check it out," Jason said just above a whisper to get Nora's attention.

She looked in his direction and saw a stone obelisk that looked almost identical to the two spires they had back at the Newell Sheriff's Office.

Nora's eyes went wide, recognizing immediately this could be the connection they'd been trying to make.

"How can I help you?" a man said, walking up to Nora and Jason as he wiped his hands with a towel.

The man was long and lean, approaching them with a quiet, purposeful stride. His frame was slender and strong, his skin sun-soaked and weathered from the elements. The man's movements were economical and efficient, like he was just in the middle of something when they walked in.

Nora and Jason both pulled their credentials out at the same time.

"I'm Nora Price, and this is my partner, Jason Snyder. We're with the FBI. Are you Orman Lamprou?"

"Yes. What's this about?" the man asked, his curiosity piqued.

"We were hoping we could speak with you for a moment about your stone obelisks," Nora answered.

"Okay," the man said, like he wasn't sure what to do with Nora's reason for being there.

"Is there somewhere we can sit down and talk?" Jason prompted.

"Sure thing. I was just about to close up. Let me flip on the door, and then we can have a seat in my office," he said, detouring around them.

"Sounds good," Jason agreed.

"Follow me," the man requested as he returned from the front of the store.

Nora and Jason followed Orman Lamprou through a plant maze littered with stone sculptures. Nora spotted two more stone obelisks along the way. She had a feeling this man wasn't the man they were looking for, but maybe he could point them in the right direction.

Orman Lamprou's office wasn't much. It looked like it had been a storage closet at one point, with barely enough room for a small steel desk and three metal chairs. A large whiteboard hung behind the desk with notes scribbled on it, none of which Nora could decipher. There was a calendar hanging to the left of the desk, but it hadn't been changed in three months.

Nora and Jason sat down as Orman Lamprou took his seat across from them.

"What do you want to know about the obelisks?" he asked, no pleasantries or mincing words.

"Who makes them?" Jason asked, already knowing the answer.

"I do. In my workshop out back."

"Are they a popular item with your customers?" Nora asked curiously.

"Yeah, they're my most popular stonework. Why?" the man asked, studying Nora and Jason with a critical eye.

Jason pulled out two photographs, one of each of the stone spires found by the victims he'd printed off from the evidence logs. They didn't want to show the man crime scene photos if they could avoid it.

"Do you recognize these?" Jason asked, sliding the two photographs in front of Orman Lamprou.

"They look like mine. Did they have the evil eye and "OL" on the bottom?" he asked after glancing at the photos.

"Yes, they did," Nora answered.

"How do your customers normally incorporate these into their landscaping?" Jason asked, the firmness of his tone indicative of the seriousness of the conversation.

"I make them for people to put in their gardens or line their patios. Things like that. I think some people have used them inside their homes as well, but I'm not really sure how."

Orman Lamprou seemed thoroughly confused. He wasn't nervous or fidgety, but he seemed to know whatever was going on was something significant. He looked back and forth between Nora and Jason like he was waiting for someone to tell him what was going on.

"What's the significance of the Evil Eye?" Nora questioned.

"I'm Greek. It's for protection."

"Protection?" Jason wondered aloud, more to himself than to Nora or Orman Lamprou.

"Yes. I make and sell things to create beautiful spaces, which can inspire jealousy or envy in others. The Evil Eye helps repel things like that. Or at least that's what my Ya-ya always used to say," the man explained, a flatness to his tone. Then, he asked, "Are either of you going to tell me why you're asking me about my obelisks?"

"The two photos you're looking at are from two crime scenes. These obelisks were left with the victims," Nora replied. She watched him absorb the information she'd just shared with him.

First, a wave of shock washed over Orman Lamprou's face, like he could not believe what he was hearing. Then, his thick, dark brows furrowed as he understood the words she'd just said.

"Crime scenes?" he stammered.

"Yes, they were found at two different locations. The suspect appears to be leaving them as some sort of message," Nora expounded, careful to not give too much away.

"Sweet Jesus," the man groaned, floored by the revelation his sculptures were now part of an ongoing criminal investigation.

"Do you have any idea who might have bought these from you?" Jason asked, pointing at the two photos.

"Umm... I can't believe any of my customers would break the law, let alone hurt someone. I can't... this is some kind of sick joke, right? Is someone trying to punk me or something?" the man asked, suddenly looking around for hidden cameras.

"No, Mr. Lamprou. We're trying to find out who killed two people and left your obelisks with the bodies," Nora sighed.

"Can you think of anyone you've sold these to recently who might have seemed... off?" Jason probed.

"I have no idea who could have done the things you're talking about. It's sick. That's just... no. I don't have a clue," the man admitted softly, anguish taking over.

"Do you have a list of customers who purchased your obelisks recently we could take a look at?" Nora interjected.

"I only accept cash. I can't afford all those fees to take credit or debit cards, and no one has checks anymore."

"The obelisks aren't lightweight. If someone bought them and had them delivered, you'd have their addresses, right?" Jason asked, hopeful.

"I don't deliver."

Nora watched Orman Lamprou's body language shift with each question. There was something he wasn't telling them.

"What are you not telling us, Mr. Lamprou?" Nora pressed, her tone firm and accusatory.

"I... I don't..." the man stuttered.

"We're trying to solve two murders and catch this killer before they kill anyone else. If you know something, or even just *suspect* something, now's the time to talk," Nora urged.

"A couple of weeks ago, a man came in and wanted to buy several of these obelisks," the man said, pointing to the photos.

Nora wasn't sure what to ask first – more about the man or how many obelisks he bought.

"Okay..." Jason said, encouraging Orman Lamprou to continue the story.

"He was... different... than my other customers. He stood out. I thought he was just going to ask for directions or something, and then he said he wanted to buy thirteen granite obelisks."

"Thirteen?" Nora repeated, terrified she'd heard the man correctly.

"Yeah. He wiped out what I had."

"You mentioned he stood out. What about him was so... memorable?" Jason questioned.

"He had this shaggy, greasy mop of black hair, but it looked dyed. It was so dark compared to how pale his skin was. And he was covered, head to toe, in black. At first, I thought he was in a costume or something, but it seemed too early for that kind of thing," Orman Lamprou described.

"So, he looked sort of gothic or something?" Nora asked, trying to get a clearer picture.

"Yes, exactly. He paid cash and picked them up two days later."

"Given the size and materials of the obelisks, I assume that was a significant sale," Nora pointed out, her tone thinly veiled with insinuation.

"Yes, it was."

"You said he picked them up later. Did he leave a name or phone number for you to contact him?"

"No. I'm the only one here, so I knew who he was when he came back," the man shrugged.

"Is there anything else about this man you can recall that might help us identify him?" Nora asked, frustration underlining her every word.

"Maybe. When he picked up the obelisks, he didn't have his arms covered and I saw a tattoo on his right forearm."

"What did it look like," Jason asked, pulling out his notepad to write down the description.

"It was an obelisk with a pentagram on the front, and it had two words. I think they were some other language, something old like Latin. When I asked him about it, he said it was for the 'temple of the thirteen'," the man shrugged, like he wasn't sure if he was being helpful or not.

"Thank you, Mr. Lamprou," Nora said as she and Jason stood up. She had no idea if anything he'd told them would lead them to their suspect, but it was a lead. And it could bring them closer to their killer.

CHAPTER THIRTEEN

Royce Kimball stared out at the dark blue water lapping at the seawall of Twisp Harbor. The clouds hung in the air like someone had painted them there, the late afternoon sky a perfect backdrop. The view was one of the reasons he'd picked this apartment, and it never failed to deliver a spectacular sight no matter what time of day it was.

He'd always loved to swim in the ocean when he was growing up. But that had changed ten years ago to the day. He'd gone for a swim with friends in the harbor and almost drowned.

Well, he actually did drown. When the paramedics arrived on the scene, he had no pulse. They worked in tandem to resuscitate him, and it took over two minutes before he regained consciousness. He'd only been twenty-two at the time, and he'd thought for sure that would be the worst thing that would ever happen to him.

Then, two months ago, he'd faced death again when his apartment building caught fire. A neighbor had left something cooking in hot grease on the stove while they went to check on their kids in the other room. They only meant to be gone for a minute, but then they'd gotten a phone call.

When they came back, the stove and cabinets above it were engulfed in flames. The neighbor hadn't known what to do, so they threw water on the fire, thinking it would put it out. Instead, it was like dousing the flames in gasoline.

At the time, Royce had been working non-stop double shifts at the hospital for almost two weeks. He'd come home and collapsed on the couch, too exhausted to even eat. When the apartment below him was ravaged by flames and smoke, he was dead to the world, oblivious to what was going on around him. He'd removed the battery from the smoke detector a couple of days before and had forgotten to replace it, so by the time he awoke, choking from the smoke and heat, he was certain his time had finally run out.

But he'd been wrong. Again. Firemen pulled him out of the blaze with minor burns and acute respiratory distress, but he was still alive. He could not believe it.

Royce wondered how he got so lucky, how he was still standing after two near-death incidents. He also could not help but wonder if he'd still see the world for all its beauty the way he did now if it hadn't almost been taken from him twice.

A sudden knock on his front door interrupted his thoughts. He looked at his watch. It was almost six, which was too late for package delivery services in his area. Royce wondered if his neighbor, Eileen, had locked herself out of her apartment again.

He walked over to the door and peered out of the peephole. A man with a wild mess of short dark curls stood patiently in the hall. Royce could not place him, but something about him seemed familiar.

He opened the door with a warm smile. "Can I help you?"

"I hope so. I'm looking for Royce Kimball," he said, his tone optimistic.

"That's me." Royce shrugged with a smile.

"Perfect. I'm from the insurance adjuster's office investigating the fire at the Wilkins Apartments this summer. Do you have a minute to review and sign a couple of affidavits?" the man asked, holding up a manila envelope.

"Oh yeah, I think I remember someone saying you'd be coming by. Come on in," Royce said, gesturing for the man to follow him inside.

"Thank you, Mr. Kimball. This is a great place you have here, a great place to regroup," the man observed.

"Yes, I feel very lucky to be here. Can you believe this was the second time in the last ten years I almost died?" Royce said, bewilderment on his face.

"Wow, that is... lucky," the man agreed. Royce noted something odd in the man's tone with how he said 'lucky'. It seemed almost sour, like the word was a bitter pill he could not get out of his mouth fast enough.

"You said you needed me to sign something?" Royce prompted, suddenly uncomfortable with the stranger standing in front of him.

"Yes, I do. But it appears I've dropped my pen somewhere along the way," the man said as he checked his pockets and looked around. Something about his movements seemed rehearsed.

"Oh. I'm sure I have a pen somewhere. Let me see what I can find," Royce offered.

He remembered seeing a pen on the counter by the fridge the night before, so he turned to walk through the living room towards the kitchen. Out of nowhere, he felt a sharp whack to the back of his head, and the beauty of Twisp Harbor before him snapped to black.

Royce slowly blinked his eyes open, his head throbbing and his eyesight blurry. He blinked a few more times, trying to make them focus. Once he started to make out shapes, he realized he wasn't in his home anymore. Nothing looked familiar. He tried to move, but something was holding him in place.

"I was starting to think I'd hit you too hard," a man's voice called out to him. Royce's brain seemed to be short-circuiting. He could not make sense of what was going on.

Who what this guy? What did he want?

Questions overwhelmed him, but he could not seem to connect what he was thinking with his mouth to ask them out loud.

"What?" Royce finally asked the only word he could manage.

"There isn't going to be anyone here to save you this time, Mr. Kimball. You've stolen enough time from the rest of us, and I'm going to make sure you never take another minute that doesn't belong to you," the man hissed as he lowered himself on top of Royce's body, further pinning him to the ground.

The weight of the man on his chest felt like he was being crushed by an anvil. Panic tore through Royce like a lightning strike, the adrenaline rush forcing him to fight back, understanding in an instant that this man meant him grave harm. He tried to move his arms and legs, but he could not. He was trapped.

"What are you doing?" Royce forced out as he struggled to breathe, his eyes wide with terror.

The man leaned down over him so that they were eye-to-eye and grimaced. It was a horrifying expression – one Royce had never seen on any face before.

"I'm restoring the balance, thief," the man snarled.

Royce realized the only thing he had was his voice. He opened his mouth to cry out for help as loudly as he could, but it was no use. The man wrapped both hands tightly around his throat and squeezed, cutting off his pleas before they ever got started.

The man was right. No one was coming to save him. No one even knew he needed saving.

Royce felt pressure building in his skull, an urgency to get air to his lungs bursting beneath his skin. He flailed beneath the man, hoping somehow to knock him off long enough to catch his breath.

But the more he tried, the more pressure pushed against his insides, like all of his organs were desperate to escape his failing body all at once. His vision blurred with black spots, and he knew this was it. This time, he wasn't going to be so lucky.

CHAPTER FOURTEEN

Nora scanned the page of images and clicked the arrow to go to the next page. So far, she hadn't found anything in the FBI's tattoo database that looked like the tattoo Orman Lamprou had described. There were hundreds of thousands of photos of tattoos to search, all collected from various law enforcement agencies over more than a decade, but the search function wasn't user-friendly.

"This is going to take forever," Jason complained.

They'd agreed she'd start her search at the beginning of the database, and he'd start at the end, working his way backwards.

"How many pages have you gone through so far?" she asked as she dipped a breadstick into marinara sauce and took a bite.

One of the officers ordered some kind of pizza party pack while they were at Stone & Bloom and had leftovers. Nora was grateful they didn't mind sharing. She and Jason were starving but had too much to do to stop and get something to eat.

"Seventeen of a billion," he grumbled.

"Any obelisks?"

"None," Jason sighed.

He rolled his chair back, stood up, and stretched. Nora knew he hated this part of their work, but it was the part that helped them solve cases.

"If you wanted to take a quick break, go for a walk or whatever, I could use a fresh cup of coffee," she suggested, knowing he was getting too antsy to concentrate.

"Yeah?"

"Yeah," she nodded, reassuring him. They'd been operating on almost no sleep, pushing hard to get the two murders solved before there could be another one. Something had to give.

"Detective Wakefield said that place around the corner had good coffee and pastries. Maybe I'll go there and get us something stronger than the ground stuff they're percolating in the break room."

"What place around the corner?" Nora asked. She had no idea what Jason was talking about.

"The Daily Mugshot, which, by the way, is a great name for a coffee place located near the local police station," Jason opined with a thoughtful grin.

"No kidding," Nora agreed. Then, she added for good measure, "I don't want any of that fancy stuff like a cappuccino or whatever. I just want hot, strong coffee with whole milk and two sugars."

"Price, I've known you for over five years. I think I know what kind of coffee you like," Jason huffed.

Nora rolled her eyes at him. He was right – he should know her coffee order. But that didn't stop him from getting her all kinds of frou-frou drinks whenever she wasn't clear about what she wanted. He was always trying to get her to try new things, which was fine with some stuff. Just not with her coffee.

"I shouldn't be long, but text me if you find anything," he said over his shoulder as he left the conference room.

Nora leaned back in her chair and stretched her legs out in front of her. If she was honest with herself, she'd admit she needed a break, too. But she never wanted to appear like she was slacking off, especially in front of Jason. She felt like he would not respect her as much if she didn't work as hard as she did.

But her drive for constant achievement had nothing to do with Jason and everything to do with her missing sister. For fourteen years, she'd had this other person who was more beautiful, smarter, more everything that she was, and everyone she knew compared her to Sophia.

Maybe, in time, she would've grown out of that resentment, or at least worked through it. But she never got the chance. Nora wondered what Sophia would think of her if she'd seen who she'd become after the abduction.

Would she be proud of me?

Nora found herself asking this question more often lately, and something inside of her doubted her sister – or even her parents – would be impressed with the work she did. She'd solved more than thirty cases, but that didn't matter to them. At the end of the day, Nora had failed to do the one thing she'd set out to do when she joined the FBI – figure out what happened to her and her sister when they were teenagers and bring Sophia home.

Nora sighed loudly, grateful there wasn't anyone around to hear it. She checked her phone to see if her mom or Dane had reached out, but there were no messages. She typed up a quick message to her mom and hit send.

Hi there. Working a case right now, but wanted to check in. I hope everything is okay. Love you.

Nora copied the text, removed the loving sentiment at the end, and then sent it to Dane. Hopefully, one or both of them would respond so she'd know they're all right. She imagined both of them had struggled with the news of Trudie Whittier's sudden death, especially given the nature of how the woman died.

In fact, Nora knew if she stopped long enough to think about it, she would be struggling herself. But she didn't stop. She could not.

Nora's only method of survival was distraction. She drove herself into the ground, guaranteeing she'd never have time to think about all the things she'd been through over the years. It's also why she had such dreadful nightmares. It all caught up to her in the end.

She forced herself back to the tattoo search, disinterested in any more self-analysis. After clicking through several more pages, she decided to try a different angle. She opened a browser search bar and typed in the description of the tattoo.

Nothing came up.

Then, she typed in "Temple of the Thirteen" to see what that would yield. Almost immediately a list of websites and images populated. She scrolled down, looking for something that might resemble any part of the information Orman Lamprou had given them.

Nora clicked forward to the next page, and there, at the top, was a website for "Malum Tredecim". There was no descriptors next to the two words, but something in her gut said she needed to click on the site.

As the site loaded, an image at the top caught Nora's eye. An obelisk with a pentagram on the front sat between the words "Malum" and "Tredecim". She pulled out her phone and snapped a photo of just the obelisk.

Then, in another tab, she searched for the phone number for Stone & Bloom. Nora tapped the number and lifted the phone to her ear.

"Stone and Bloom, this is Orman. How can I help?" a man answered on the second ring.

"Hi, Mr. Lamprou. This is Agent Price with the FBI. I think I might have found an image of the tattoo you described. Do you have a number I can text you the picture or an email address?" Nora asked, her voice charged with anticipation.

"Of course. Send it to my phone. Six, one, seven. Five, five, five. Five, three, two, one," he said.

"Thanks. I'll send it now. Please confirm either way," she asked.

"No problem," he agreed.

Nora sent Orman Lamprou the picture and waited for him to respond. Within a matter of seconds, she received his reply.

Yes. That's it.

Nora about jumped out of her seat with excitement. They *finally* had a lead. She thanked the man for his help and then started to text Jason with the good news.

"Head's up, Price," he said, startling her as he walked in with a drink tray with two waters and two travel cups of coffee.

"I was just about to text you. We've got a lead," she said, eager for him to see what she'd stumbled upon.

"See what happens when I'm not here to bug you," he teased as he set her drinks in front of her. Then, he added, "Show me what you've got."

"I got tired of looking in the database, so I tried doing a web search for the Temple of the Thirteen. This came up, so I reached out and confirmed with Orman Lamprou that this is what the tattoo he saw looks like," she explained, pointing to the website on her computer.

"Huh," he muttered.

"Huh, what?" Nora asked, unsure why Jason wasn't as elated as she was.

"Well, Orman Lamprou said the guy told him the words meant 'the Temple of the Thirteen'...".

"Yeah, so?" Nora interrupted, not following him.

"So, my Latin is rusty, but there's no way *Malum Tredecim* means what that guy said it means," he said pointedly.

"Yeah, I don't think *malum* means 'temple'," Nora agreed, looking back at the website.

She opened another tab, searched for a translation tool, and typed in the term to see what it meant.

"The Evil Thirteen," she read aloud.

"That sounds fun," he said sarcastically.

Nora clicked back on the website and started scrolling through it as Jason looked over her shoulder.

"By scythe and sickle, we Krononites stand united against all who would do us harm. We serve Tartarus and embrace our most carnal needs and primal instincts. Leave your hope at the door," Nora read from the webpage.

"Is that a Dante reference?" Jason asked, sounding surprised.

"Something like that," Nora nodded.

"I'll see what I can dig up on these folks while you look through the site. This group doesn't sound run-of-the-mill, if you know what I mean," Jason said, sitting down at his computer and logging on.

"No kidding," Nora agreed.

Nora checked out the rest of the site as she sipped on her coffee. There were several blog posts about what it meant to be a Krononite, which read a lot like sections of a manifesto. The more she reviewed the writings on the site, the more the Krononites seemed like a cult.

"I found some posts online warning people to stay away from the *Evil Thirteen*, claiming it was a front for a Satanic-like cult," Jason announced.

"I'm getting that vibe, too, but nothing concrete," Nora said, recounting what she'd found so far.

"Well, two different people talk about goat sacrifices, and a third person mentions some kind of weird animal orgy."

"Oh wow," Nora shook her head, her eyebrows raised in mild surprise. "This was definitely not on my bingo card for this case," she added with a scoff.

"Do they have an address on their site?" Jason asked, disregarding her comment.

"Yeah, it looks like they're in Mill Creek, which is the next town over," Nora answered after checking the site.

"I think we should coordinate with Detective Wakefield and the Mill Creek police before we pay these Malum Tredecim Krononites a visit," Jason suggested.

By the looks of their website, Nora agreed they were going to need some extra help. This cult could very well be harboring their killer.

CHAPTER FIFTEEN

"What time did Detective Wakefield say Detective Knapp was going to get here? It's kind of late," Jason said pointedly, checking his watch.

"Any time now," Nora sighed.

"Will it just be the four of us storming the castle, or are they bringing backup?"

Nora shrugged.

Jason didn't like how scattered this plan was. They needed more structure, more security in the next steps they were about to take. He had no interest charging in on some crazy cult and having another Waco or Jonestown situation on their hands.

"Maybe we should gear up while we wait," he suggested. He wasn't good at being idle, something he and Nora had in common.

"Are we just running in guns blazing or what?" she challenged, picking up on his anxiety.

"I don't know, Nora," he fussed.

Nora put her hands up, as if to say, *Whoa*. He sighed again, his frustration mounting.

"We could just have them meet us there. It might save some time," he proposed, wanting to do something more than stand around and wait.

"Sorry for your wait, Agent Snyder. Agent Price. This is Detective Knapp," Detective Wakefield said as he walked in before Nora could respond.

Nora stood up and joined Jason as they shook hands with Detective Knapp. He was a short, rotund man with a buzz cut and big attitude. His face was beet red, like he'd been running or yelling at someone and didn't have enough air to do either.

"Thank you for coming out tonight, Detective Knapp. Since this is your territory, what can you tell us about Temple of the Thirteen?" Jason asked, doing his best not to match the man's energy. Nora always told him she thought it was so easy for him to be charming or diplomatic, but the truth was it was a constant struggle.

Men like Detective Knapp made Jason want to punch first and ask questions later. They acted like they were superior, somehow better than everyone else because they had a Detective shield. More often than not, though, Jason knew getting those shields in small towns was based more on politics than merit.

"They've been around for a few years now. They seem fairly harmless. I think the most we've ever had was a noise complaint," the man shrugged.

"The group might not be the problem, but someone within the group could be a killer," Nora pointed out, her cheeks reddening. Jason noticed she slid her fists into her pockets, white knuckles and all, as she spoke. She was always so reactive.

"Might? Could? Is that the language the FBI uses nowadays?" Detective Knapp sneered.

Nora plastered a placating grin on her face, and Jason knew he better speak up before she did.

"I understand your apprehension, Detective. It's just we already have two murders, and I'd hate for there to be a third one in your town because we didn't take this seriously," Jason cautioned.

The red-faced detective's face fell as he realized the implication could have on someone in his position.

"They do a lot of all-nighter type raves. I can call up some guys to meet us there and we can go in under the guise of a noise complaint," the detective offered.

Nora made eye contact with Jason, nodding in approval at the man's sudden cooperative change of heart.

"Sounds like a plan. We'll follow you," Jason directed.

Jason and Nora followed the two detectives in an unmarked sedan to Mill Creek, a small town less than ten minutes outside of Newell. Their headlights lit up the night in front of them, but otherwise, everything around them was covered in darkness.

The sleepy two-lane road leading them towards the Temple of the Thirteen morphed from a smooth black in Newell to a cracked and patched grey the closer they got to Mill Creek. Just as they passed a faded green highway sign welcoming them to the town, the detectives' vehicles in front of them suddenly turned right. Jason pulled onto a dusty dirt road after them, wondering where they were going.

"This just got interesting," Nora commented.

"Yep. Glad we already put our vests on," Jason agreed.

Jason followed the detectives until they got to a clearing where several black and white cop cars were waiting for them. Off to the right, Jason noticed a large, run-down factory. There weren't any outside lights, but he could hear a loud base thumping under a dark night sky.

Jason and Nora checked their weapons before they got out of the car and joined the detectives with their men.

"What do we know?" Detective Knapp asked his men, looking at each of them for an answer.

"I saw a few people go in wearing long, dark robes. When the door opened, there were neon-styled lights, but no other identifiers," one officer said.

"There's definitely some type of party or something going on," another one piped up.

"All right. Everyone got their vests?" the detective asked.

"Yes, sir," they said in unison. Nora and Jason nodded as well, an automatic response to the question.

Jason didn't like raids. They were dangerous and unpredictable, especially when the people leading them weren't experienced.

"Anyone know what the layout inside looks like?" Jason asked, hoping the group of officers was more prepared than they looked.

"I used to come here when it was a make-out spot. It's two stories with at least four exits – two in the front, two in the back," a pale-faced, dark-haired officer answered.

Well, that's better than nothing, I guess, Jason thought to himself.

He caught Nora's eye, and he could see she was worried, too.

"Okay. You take three guys with you to the back two exits and we'll take the front," Detective Knapp ordered.

The officers nodded and all turned towards the ominous looking building just up ahead in the distance. The hulking silhouette loomed like an unknown beast waiting in the shadows for them. Jason hoped they didn't regret this as he fell in line behind the locals.

"I need you at my six, Price," he whispered to Nora when she moved up to where he was in the line. She immediately fell back. He was grateful she knew he wanted her at his back because he trusted her and not for any other archaic, patriarchal reason.

The officers split up as they arrived at the front of the building, half moving around one side and the other half moving around the other. The two detectives remained at the front with Jason and Nora. Once everyone was in place, Detective Knapp screamed, "Go!" as loudly as he could.

Adrenaline shot through Jason like an arrow as he surged forward into the building. Black lights lined the walls with all kinds of UV-reactive murals lighting up around them. The colors were bright and disorienting.

"FBI!" Jason shouted as the police descended in unison into the building.

"Police!" Detective Knapp's men shouted.

Suddenly, there were shrieks and screams coming from every direction as people rushed towards the exits, desperate to escape risk of prosecution.

"Hold your ground," Detective Knapp shouted at his men. Jason wasn't sure anyone could hear him over the loud electronic dance beats thrumming through the place.

The music abruptly stopped, and all Jason could hear was chaos. People wrapped in white bed sheets reminiscent of togas were clambering from every direction to get out of the building. It looked like a busted frat party. The officers blocked their getaway, handguns and tasers drawn at the ready.

"Everyone get down on the ground, now!" Detective Knapp shouted, his voice booming across the concrete and metal building. People dropped to the ground at his command, and the chaos quickly came to an end.

"Impressive," Nora acknowledged quietly as she stood next to Jason, as she surveyed the people who were now under arrest. This was no frat party. There were men and women of all ages, from young, shapely females in their twenties to older men with salt-and-pepper hair. All races, all ages . . . it was a motley assortment. The only thing they had in common was their white garb.

Once the police had the building under siege and its inhabitants under arrest, Jason and Nora began to look around.

There were strange UV-reactive paintings of a godlike monster eating small beings on one wall, a poor attempt to depict the myth about the titan, Kronos, eating his children.

"At least we know we got the right place," Jason said, nodding at the wall.

Nora rolled her eyes and shook her head. He knew exactly what she was thinking: *could this get any weirder*?

"This place reminds me of the other crime scenes," Nora pointed out as they climbed the stairs to the second floor.

Jason glanced about, nodding in agreement. It was old and abandoned, a skeleton of a building just waiting for someone to come by and leave a body for them to find.

The second floor had a large opening to down below where Nora and Jason could see the officers handcuffing people Jason assumed were cult members and guests. A large walkway surrounding the opening with rooms off shooting from each corner. They checked each one, hoping something would finally connect this place to their investigation.

Jason noticed in the last room, there was a strange break in the paneling on the far right wall. He moved closer to check it out and realized it was a hidden door. There wasn't any indication of how to open the door, so he pressed on the wall to see if it was on a pressure hinge. Sure enough, it popped right open.

"How'd you know to do that?" Nora asked curiously.

"Just a guess, like almost everything I do," he replied sarcastically.

Nora rolled her eyes again and gestured for him to go first. He was surprised she wasn't shoving him aside to see what was behind the door.

Jason put his hand at his side, the cool metal of his gun easing his mind. A set of battery-operated work lights sat off in the corner of what appeared to be some sort of sanctuary-type space. Two rows of wooden pews sat in front of them, with an aisle leading to an altar below a hanging metal pentagram.

"Look," Nora gasped as she pointed off to the left.

Jason followed her direction, his nerves fraying at the tension. There, sitting in a line, side-by-side, were the obelisks from Orman Lamprou's garden décor shop. Jason hurried over to the stone spires to see if they were two short, proof they were finally on the right track.

As he approached, he began counting the obelisks.

Thirteen.

Jason looked at Nora, knowing he'd find the disappointment he felt on her face.

If there are thirteen here, how could this be the same guy?

It was a good question, one that had to be asked. But it was also evidence they weren't really on the right track after all. They still had a killer on the loose, and he was bound to strike again soon.

CHAPTER SIXTEEN

Nora leaned against the unmarked sedan next to Jason. They watched as Temple of the Thirteen members were led in handcuffs out of the old factory, a van waiting to take them off to the county jail. They weren't killers. They weren't even actual cult members.

After Nora and Jason found the obelisks, they'd talked to Malachi Stone, the leader of the group. He'd purchased the obelisks, and he had an alibi for both murders.

It turned out, the Temple of the Thirteen was some kind of online gaming group who liked to get together after beating a level and role play some of the scenes from the game. Everything they'd seen online related to the group was all just fiction, conjured fantasies from a group of gaming fanatics who were trying to bring their characters to life. Even the "witness accounts" were fake.

"They certainly seemed dangerous," Nora commented, trying to make herself feel better.

"They still broke the law. They shouldn't have been here," Jason grumbled.

"True. At least Detective Knapp sees this as a win," Nora sighed.

While the Temple of the Thirteen members weren't in a cult, they were partaking and dealing in illicit substances, something the town had charged Detective Knapp with cracking down on. Now, he could say he'd done just that.

Overall, it was a win-win situation for him. He'd managed to catch a group of disorderly miscreants wreaking havoc on his small town and embarrass two FBI agents at the same time. Nora never liked wearing egg on her face, and she knew Jason liked it even less.

"Yeah," Jason agreed, his mood sour.

"You know, I hate to say it, but..." Nora started.

"Then, don't say it," Jason interrupted.

She sighed again. She understood he was just as frustrated as she was, but she also knew that part of the problem was they were running on caffeine fumes. They were trying to solve this case on a wing and a prayer, and it was catching up to them. They could not keep pushing so hard without there being consequences.

"Look, you and I both know we're doing everything we can to close this case. But that shouldn't include trying to make it a hundred miles on an empty tank. We've got to figure out how to take a more measured approach. *Both* of us. Because at the end of the day, we're riding too close to the line where things get missed and start getting sloppy, Jason. And that's the last thing either of us wants."

"We should head back to Newell," he said as he pushed his body off of the car, ignoring her plea. He wasn't usually the moody one, and she didn't like how the tables were turning.

It wasn't like Jason had had an easy life. He'd had drama growing up like most people. But he hadn't been through anything close to what she'd faced, and until now, he'd always been respectful of that difference.

"Don't be that guy," Nora warned.

"What guy?" Jason challenged.

"All broody and morose because something isn't going your way. We've always been able to be straight with each other. Stop treating me like I don't know how awful this feels," she snapped.

Jason shook his head, aggravation lining his face. Nora felt her rage slowly seeping up from her gut like a Burmese Python.

"Did you hear me?" she asked, irritated with his sudden impertinence of his attitude.

"You're not telling me anything I don't know, Nora. It's late. You're tired. I'm tired. And we still don't have a lead."

"So, what do you propose?" she asked, her tone growing more acidic.

"I don't know. Maybe we should just go back to Newell and see if we can get a few hours' sleep before we have to get up and start all over," he shrugged before getting in the car, slamming the door shut, and cranking the ignition.

Nora looked back at the scene of flashing blue and white lights and so many people in handcuffs just for wanting to have a good time.

What a waste, she thought.

Nora could not help but wonder if she was losing her edge, finally burning out like a flawed roman candle that never burst into the glittering fragments of light, but instead fizzled out into a trail of smoke no one could see against the dark sky.

It was bound to happen at some point.

She and Jason had put away thirty-four creeps together over the last five-almost-six years. They'd seen a lot of terrible things and solved cases that would make someone even with the strongest constitution look away.

There was something about this case that seemed to be harder than the others, although Nora could not put her finger on exactly what it was. The puzzle wasn't coming together, the clues weren't falling in line. They were hitting dead ends at every turn.

She also wondered if he was getting tired of dealing with all of her issues and leftover childhood trauma. It wasn't like she'd asked for any of the problems she'd had. She wished every day that it had been Sophia who returned all those years ago, not her. She could not help but feel that way, but she also knew that could not be easy for Jason to deal with on a daily basis.

Maybe five years was the sweet spot for partners. She had no idea. Jason had been her first and only partner since she joined the force. She could not imagine working with anyone else, but she also could not picture them continuing on like this.

Nora looked around one last time before she got in the car. Jason didn't say anything to her as she shut the door and buckled her seatbelt, which only irritated her more. As he turned around and headed down the dark dirt road back towards Newell, Nora knew they something had to give.

She started to try and talk to him again but decided against it when she noticed how hard he was clenching his jaw. Instead, she quietly slipped her phone from her pocket to see if she had any missed calls or texts.

No messages. No leads. No threads to pull.

She started to wonder if the evening could get any worse when both of their phones chimed. She looked at hers and groaned.

"They found another body."

CHAPTER SEVENTEEN

Jason turned into the parking lot for Twisp Harbor and Freight, an old Navy shipyard that had been shut down for years. Cop cars lined the front of the building while the medical examiner's van sat off to the right, all the vehicles still running with their lights on. Nora checked her phone again and realized they still had just a little over an hour before sunrise.

She made a mental note to check the other victims' files again. Nora could not recall the official times of death for Boyd Ewen or Lynna McLean, but maybe there was something there.

The rust-streaked skeleton of the shipyard building loomed over the dark harbor, with shadows of towering cranes that stood like frozen sentinels, their oxidized arms reaching towards the late-night sky. Nora could hear the water lapping at what was likely wooden pilings as she stepped out of the car, but it was still too dark for her to make them out.

"Agent Snyder? Agent Price?" a middle-aged man in a crisp suit asked as he approached them.

They nodded in unison.

"I'm Detective Noyes with the Twisp Harbor Sheriff's Office. I'll fill you in," he said as he gestured for them to walk with him.

"Is this the same M.O.?" Nora asked, too tired to wait for the detective to dive into whatever backstory he'd discovered before they'd arrived.

"It is. The victim is Royce Kimball. Male. Early 30s. He was killed earlier this evening and found by Finn Harrison, a local building inspector. He's still on scene, and we've left everything as it was when he found it."

"Good," Jason said, his tone clipped.

Nora swiped a glance at her partner. Even when he was frustrated with her, he was still usually overly polite to everyone else.

"You good?" she asked under her breath, trying not to call him out in front of the detective. Thankfully, the detective wasn't paying any attention.

"As good as I'm going to get at five in the morning," he snarled.

Nora sighed loudly, her way of warning Jason to get a grip. Regardless of whatever issues he had with her, which she still didn't understand, he still needed to act professional.

"Right this way," the detective directed them before Nora could say anything else to her partner.

The tension between them did not ease up as they made their way under the crime scene tape and into the building.

Nora was surprised to find the inside of the shipyard free of any debris and clean, especially in comparison to the dilapidated shell housing the space. In fact, she smelled something faintly reminiscent of fresh paint. The detective's flashlight wasn't enough to see much about the place, but the shipyard definitely did not quite align with the other two crime scenes in disrepair.

"Is that paint?" she finally asked when the smell got stronger as they walked farther into the building.

"You have an excellent sense of smell," the detective complimented.

"Thanks," Nora replied with a tight smile. Jason continued his silent tantrum and said nothing.

"The building was recently purchased, which is why the inspector was here," the detective explained.

"Is it normal for the inspector to be here before dawn?" Jason asked, finally contributing more than just a mute attitude.

"Mr. Harrison likes to start his day early," the detective answered, a familiarity lingering in how he spoke about the inspector.

Nora started to say something but changed her mind. They walked down a crude, narrow hallway that looked like it had been built to keep people from having to deal with the elements during harsher weather patterns. It connected a larger building with a much smaller pole building, which was also makeshift in its construction.

"Here we are," the detective announced as they arrived at the crime scene. Nora almost laughed out loud at the number of people standing around, contaminating the scene. She looked at Jason, wondering if he noticed the absurdity, but he just looked straight ahead.

Several crime scene technicians buzzed about collecting evidence while a uniformed officer talked to a man with a look of complete horror on his face.

That must be the inspector, Nora thought to herself.

She started to walk over to the man when she noticed the scene was different than the last two murders. The body and obelisk were in the same position, but this time there was a small lantern to the left, which created an elongated shadow behind the obelisk. The lantern had a marker beside it, which meant it was *evidence*.

"That's new," Nora muttered.

"Pardon?" the detective asked, like he thought Nora was saying something to him.

"She wasn't talking to you," Jason snapped.

The detective's eyes widened with surprise, and he quickly excused himself to go speak with the medical examiner.

"Was that necessary?" Nora asked her partner.

"It's a clock," Jason announced, again ignoring her question, as he moved closer to the body.

"Jason," she called after him. When he didn't respond, she tried again. "Agent Snyder."

Finally, he stopped and sighed. Then, in one smooth movement, he turned to face her.

"Yes, Agent Price?" he asked, his voice cold, his face stone.

It took everything Nora had not to scream at him for acting so ridiculously. She'd never seen him glower to this level, and she was done putting up with it. She marched three steps towards him so he was close enough to hear what she had to say. If he wanted to act like a child, she'd treat him like one.

"If you don't pull yourself together and start acting like my partner, Jason Snyder, so help me God, I will call Durham as soon as we're back in town and demand a transfer," she threatened in a harsh whisper.

Jason looked at her like she'd just slapped him across the face.

"What?" he asked, completely caught off guard, his ego retreating.

"You heard me." She scowled. Then, she pushed past him, not willing to engage any further, and eager to see if the obelisk was serving as some kind of crude clock.

The more she looked at the obelisk and the lantern, the more she realized Jason was right. The killer had created a makeshift sundial using an artificial light source.

How did we miss this?

Nora didn't like how often she seemed to be asking that question lately. It wasn't indicative of their normal working patterns or how they'd managed to solve so many cases together over the last five years.

As much as she wanted to hash it out with Jason and figure out what was off between them, she knew now wasn't the time. They had another body, which meant there would be more pressure from their bosses and the towns that had called them in to help to solve this case. Nora cleared her mind and focused all of her attention on the scene in front of her.

She walked around the body, making a large circle. Then, she did it again. Once she saw every angle, she understood the obelisk was only one hand on the clock. The body was the other.

"What time do you see?" she asked Jason as she looped back around, her tone crisp and impersonal.

"I don't know. Maybe eleven o'clock?" he guessed with a half-shrug.

"Eleven-thirty," she corrected. Then, she added, "The body is the second hand."

But what, exactly, did it all mean?

CHAPTER EIGHTEEN

Austen Darby watched the woman two tables over as she threw her long auburn hair back, laughing with her friends. Her joy disgusted him. No one should be allowed to steal time from others. It wasn't right.

The man had spent the morning readying the stage for the woman's demise. He'd had an array of abandoned, broken-down buildings to choose from in Carson. The once-bustling township had become practically a ghost town after the American Culinary University had relocated to another state with better incentives. The remnants of the Carson Culinary College, a local technical school that fed into the university, seemed like the perfect location.

He'd been following the woman for almost an hour around town. His presence undetected, he knew she felt him – or someone – watching. Every once in a while, he'd find her looking around, looking for the source of her discomfort. It amused him, stalking his prey, and how they never saw him coming.

Austen read through the file he'd printed up about the woman, which contained newspaper clippings, a background check, and various medical records. She'd been featured in several medical journals after she'd survived what was initially classified as a Cryptogenic stoke when they could not diagnose the cause.

It took weeks for the doctors to discover the woman had been born with a patent foramen ovale, a small flaplike opening in the wall between the upper chambers of the heart. Most people born with this congenital anomaly don't experience any complications. This woman, though, would prove to be unlike most people.

When she was twenty-one, she'd collapsed in her dorm room. She was found several hours later and rushed to the local emergency room. Apparently, the woman had flatlined several times before they were finally able to get her stable. They'd brought her back from the dead, giving her time that wasn't hers.

The whitecoats, Austen's preferred term for the incompetent medical professionals that were rampant in local hospitals, knew she'd had a stroke. They just didn't know why.

It had taken them years to understand the underlying cause of the woman's condition. When an up-and-coming cardiac fellow reviewed her case, she'd immediately identified the congenital defect and knew it was the culprit. They did surgery, and the woman was given a great prognosis.

The more Austen read, the more fury vibrated through him like a swarm of killer bees on the attack. This woman had survived something terrible, something she shouldn't have lived through, and yet here she was wasting the day away like she had all the time in the world. It was repugnant and insulting to everyone who had been taken before their time.

To make matters worse, the woman had done nothing substantial with her life. She'd never finished college, and she never stayed at a job for more than a year. There were so many others out there who had deserved to overcome sickness or to heal from terrible accidents, people who hadn't died on the table and been brought back from death. It was like she was flitting through the existence she'd been given not once, but twice.

Austen pulled out a newspaper clipping and read it for the hundredth time. The headline of the article was a gut punch, a painful reminder what he was doing was right.

Stroke Survivor Causes Fatal Crash, No Charges Filed

The woman had cheated death in her twenties only to take someone else's life – and almost her own – in her forties. The article claimed it was just an unfortunate accident. The woman had been driving home in icy conditions, and when she pulled to a stop at a red light, her car had skidded on black ice into oncoming traffic.

The woman's vehicle had collided with two other cars on the road that night. The first car she hit, the passenger survived. The second car she ran into careened into oncoming traffic, and the driver was killed instantly. By the time paramedics arrived, the woman had no pulse. They resuscitated her in the ambulance and then again in the operating room.

It was an imbalance of life of the most egregious kind. Austen didn't know the woman, but based on everything he'd learned about her, he hated her with every fiber of his being. She'd taken what was not hers, just like the others, and that he could not abide.

As he watched the woman, he wondered what Aline would think of her. Aline had always been forgiving, someone who possessed a deep well of compassion and empathy for others. She'd probably try to understand more about the woman, try to make sense of all the tragedy but Austen wasn't Aline.

He didn't care about the woman or what she'd been through. How many others should have lived in the time she'd taken? She was a thief of the worst ilk, and he could not stand by and allow her to continue to live a life that wasn't hers to live.

Austen checked his watch as the woman paid her bill. Next, she would likely go to the salon to get her hair or nails done, and then she would window shop mindlessly along main street for an hour or so. It was the only routine she had – meet with friends and pamper herself like no one else in the world mattered. He hated it. Just being within proximity to someone so selfish made him want to shower.

Everything was already set in motion before the woman had even left her house that morning. Austen had left Royce Kimball at the shipyard, positioning him and the obelisk in a way to show his next kill would be that evening around eleven-thirty.

It wasn't necessarily the exact time he would take the woman's life, but it was in the vicinity. First, he had to find the right time and place to strike. It had to be planned just so, or he could miss his opportunity altogether.

Lynna McLean and Boyd Ewen were social people, so he'd had to adjust his timelines to either late at night or very early in the morning for their deaths, so no one would see him with them. Royce Kimball was more of a homebody, so Austen could exact his justice in broad daylight without the risk of an audience. This woman, however, was the most active of his victims, which meant he had to go back to his late-night timeline to ensure success.

Austen slipped the woman's file back into his messenger bag and pulled some cash out for his bill. He'd only had a cup of coffee, but the server hadn't been a nuisance like others had been in the past. He left a ten-dollar bill under his cup and stood up, watching the woman cross the street to the nail salon.

He made a mental note to keep an eye out for her claws later when he apprehended her. He could not afford to leave behind any evidence that would link him to her death. He still had too much to do, too many thieves to bring to justice.

CHAPTER NINETEEN

Nora read through the medical examiner's notes, her frustration giving way to despondency. Royce Kimball had been killed in the late afternoon, which Boyd Ewen's crime scene had predicted. The killer was using the obelisks and bodies to tell them when they were going to strike next.

But we missed it, Nora realized.

She sat in front of her laptop, her emotions sinking into despair that they weren't going to be able to stop this killer like they had with so many others. He'd already claimed three lives. According to the latest crime scene, he was going to likely take another that night.

Nora and Jason hadn't said much to each other once they left Twisp Harbor and Freight. Both of them had been too exhausted and miserable to try to push through and keep working on the case. So, instead of returning to the Newell Sheriff's Office, they'd checked into the Merchant's House Inn at the edge of town to get a couple of hours of sleep.

To Jason's surprise, Nora had booked them in two different rooms. With all the stress they'd been under, she knew she was likely going to have nightmares if she actually managed to fall asleep. She hadn't wanted to disturb him or deal with his concern, especially after everything that'd gone on in the last eight hours.

Nora had felt bad for not explaining her reasoning behind the separate rooms when she saw the effect it had on Jason. Initially, he'd given her a questioning look, which quickly turned to dejection. Nora had been too tired for more drama, so she'd given him a forced smile and told she'd see him in a few hours.

When he didn't respond, she just walked away. She'd felt him watching her as she retreated down the hallway to her room. She could have looked back, tried to smooth things over, but Nora had had enough. They'd been a great team for several years now, but all of a sudden that had felt like it was disintegrating. And Nora, for the life of her, could not figure out why.

Once she'd reached her room, she took a quick shower to wash the grime of the past two days off of her. She'd intended to review the case files, to check the other possible "times" the killer had left with the first two victims. However, the shower had relaxed her so much, she'd fallen asleep as soon as she laid down on the bed.

She hadn't dreamt of her sister or the dark woods that always seemed to be waiting for her in those brief hours of rest. She must've been too exhausted for that part of her mind to take over in her sleep like it had so many other times before. Regardless of how little time she'd slept, it was the respite she'd needed for a reset.

Nora hadn't confirmed a specific time with Jason for them to reconnect or set an alarm. Instead, she'd been awoken by her phone. The pinging ringtone for text notifications pierced her unconscious state, arousing her slowly from her slumber. While she'd still felt tired, she'd also felt more rational.

She'd pulled up the text messages on her phone and seen her mom had finally replied.

I can't go back to Wendy's Hope. Not after Trudie. I hope you understand.

The words had been sparse, but Nora had understood the pain lying underneath them. They'd confirmed that Nora's mother had been much more deeply affected by the loss of Trudie Whittier than Nora had realized. She'd known Trudie's suicide would be hard, but she'd also known how important it had been to her mother to have somewhere she could talk about Sophia if she'd wanted to.

Nora had typed out several responses to her mother, only to erase each one. She hadn't been sure what the right thing to say was, but she also hadn't wanted to just say nothing. Finally, after a few tries, she'd simply written *I understand* and hit send.

Over all the years that had passed since Sophia went missing, Nora had believed her parents had managed to move on to some degree. Now, she'd begun to see it had all been a farce, a façade to keep up appearances. The realization had brought an awareness of their grief Nora hadn't been prepared for, but also a glimmer of hope that she didn't have to keep doing everything on her own.

Just as Nora had finished texting her mother, a message came through from Jason.

In the lobby. Ready to go when you are.

Nora hadn't responded. His words felt too impersonal, too trite. It had only made her angry all over again. Then, she'd taken a couple of deep breaths and decided she wasn't going to do the back-and-forth with him. They had too much work to do, and by the timetable the killer had set, not nearly enough time to do it in.

Nora had barely acknowledged Jason when she arrived in the lobby a few minutes later. She'd noticed he looked better, had more color in his face like he'd actually gotten some rest. Part of her had wanted to say something, make things better between them, but she had no idea where to start. They'd always had snippy moments, but nothing like this, nothing that had spilled out into their work lives.

Nora had been grateful the car ride to the Newell Sheriff's Office was short. She'd never liked silence, especially when there was someone else in the room with her. It was probably something that stemmed from the abduction, but Nora didn't dwell on any of her oddities enough to identify where they might have come from.

She'd done plenty of psychoanalysis session with shrinks over the years, and none of them could really say with certainty why she did the things she did. She didn't remember what had happened to her or her sister, so any triggers she might have developed from that experience were completely unknown to her. It had been frustrating for the professionals to never be able to uncover the root cause of her behavior, but no more frustrating than it had been for her.

Once they returned to the conference room at the back of the Sheriff's Office, Nora had gotten right to work. She'd started going through the case files, trying to create some sort of timeline for the murders. Jason might have done the same, but they hadn't spoken since she'd approached him in the lobby and said, "Let's go."

Nora knew their lack of communication could mean duplicate work and wasted time, but she wasn't ready to bridge the widening gap between them. She also knew if they didn't try to fix whatever had gone wrong soon, that gap would be too impossible to cross. She sighed at the thought and forced herself to focus back on her notes.

"I got you some coffee," Jason said quietly, offering a hot cup of coffee and startling Nora. She hadn't even realized he'd left the room.

"Oh, thanks," Nora said politely.

Jason sighed loudly as he returned to his chair. Then, instead of sitting down, he pulled it over to where Nora was and took a seat next to her.

"I'm sorry. I know I've been a jerk lately," he said, his words heartfelt and genuine.

Nora was surprised he apologized. She knew he wasn't the only one to blame for whatever was going on with them, but she hadn't expected him to wave the white flag just yet.

"I'm sorry, too. I know it's not easy being my partner or..." she started, but then stopped. This didn't feel like the type of spats she was used to with him. He'd just started shutting her out like she was just some random person in his life. The lack of sleep and the pressure from the case didn't help, but the way he'd acted had been so hurtful to her.

"You're right. It's not. But we're not just partners. You're my best friend, Nora, and I care about you so much. Probably more than I'd like to admit," Jason admitted, his tone full of melancholy.

"Then, why do you keep shutting me out?" Nora asked, her voice cracking at the end as her emotions got the best of her.

"I don't know... maybe because you keep shutting *me* out," he guessed with a shrug.

"What do you mean?" she asked, confused.

"Well... You find leads on your case, but you don't tell me about them until after the fact. And twice now, you've gone to these broken-down, derelict buildings where you could have been hurt or God knows what was waiting for you, and you didn't even think to ask me to go with you or tell me about it beforehand. And let's not even get into the stunt you pulled on the Osmond Wright case."

His words came out all at once, unexpectedly covering her like hot lava spewing out of a volcano. She wasn't sure what to say. He wasn't wrong, but it wasn't like she'd done it on purpose.

"I haven't been intentionally not telling you stuff, Jason," she said.

"I know. *That's* the problem!" he argued, his voice rising slightly with his irritation.

"What?" she asked, confused again.

"You're not trying to include me. It doesn't even occur to you that you *should* include me," he pointed out.

"You didn't even know me when all that stuff happened," she responded, a poor attempt to justify behavior she knew wasn't healthy or supportive of their relationship.

"You're right. I didn't. But I'm here now. I'm here when you wake up screaming from one of those god-awful nightmares, when I'm supposed to just sit there and hope you can self-soothe because I don't want to freak you out by trying to comfort you. I'm here when you black out from panic attacks, always so careful to shoulder your weight in a way others don't notice so you don't have to be embarrassed or concerned what they might think. I'm here when you launch yourself at these psychopaths like you're invincible or have some kind of death wish, when all I can do is just sit and watch you self-destruct. I'm *here*, Nora, every minute, watching you spiral and not being allowed to help or even talk about it," he huffed.

"Oh," Nora said softly, the realization of his words hitting her like a bucket of concrete.

"Yeah. *Oh.*"

She had no idea he'd felt this way or for how long he'd been keeping so much bottled inside. Here she was thinking he was pushing her away, hanging her out to dry, when, in reality, she was the one doing that to him.

"I didn't know," she confessed.

"I know. And as much as all of that has been painful to witness as your friend and partner of over five years, you threatening to walk away from me has been the most devastating. Because, yet again, there's nothing I can do to stop you. The only thing worse in this world that could happen to me would be your death, especially if it was caused by some situation I could have prevented or helped," he conceded.

Nora's heart sank. She'd never wanted to cause him distress or concern, not like this. At first, she started to tell him again how she hadn't meant to hurt him, that it hadn't even been in her purview. But that was his point. She hadn't included him in a purposeful or meaningful way.

"I'm so sorry, Jason. I had no idea, and I never should have threatened to have Durham transfer me. I just didn't realize..." she sighed, afraid if she said anything else, her emotions would overwhelm her.

Jason had always been there for her. He'd never tried to change her or make her feel like she was damaged goods. He'd defended her, championed her even, and always just asked that she show up the same way he did. But she hadn't. Maybe she didn't know how.

"I'll try to do better, but I might need your help. This is new territory for me, and I don't have a clue what I'm doing," she said, her voice choked with guilt, acknowledging that she'd really heard him.

"So, the moral of the story is we're both jerks," he teased, instantly alleviating the heaviness that had settled in the room.

"Pretty much," she agreed with a chuckle.

"All right. Enough therapy. We've got a case to solve," he declared, like it was just up to him.

"On that note, I think I know *when* our killer will strike again, but I'm not sure where," Nora stated.

"I might be able to help with that. I looked up the building records for Trask Textiles, Newell Auto Shop, and Twisp Harbor and Freight. All of the buildings have been abandoned for over a year, with each of their operations shutting down in March of last year."

"That can't be a coincidence. Right?" she asked, excited by the possibility of an actual lead.

"Right. It also looks like the owners all had their financing through the same bank, Newell Savings and Loan."

"Okay, so did the bank have something to do with them shutting down?" Nora asked, confused by the bank angle.

"Not that I can tell. It's just another thing I think will help us filter where the killer plans to take their next victim," Jason theorized.

"Makes sense. Based on the timetable I figured out from the other two cases, it looks like the killer is planning for a late-night murder," Nora shared.

"So, eleven-thirty at night, then?"

"Yep," she confirmed.

"I'll send you the list of buildings I found in the area that potentially fit the criteria this killer is using, so we can divide and conquer. It's pretty short with both of us working on it," Jason said as he moved his chair back in front of his computer and took a seat.

"Sounds good, partner," she nodded.

There were four buildings total for them to check out. Nora took the first two, and Jason took the last. All four buildings had the Newell Savings and Loan connection, but only one had been shut down since May of the prior year.

"I've got it," Jason announced suddenly.

"What?"

“Batch Brewery in Tarry Bay,” he said, reading his computer screen.

Nora checked the time. It was still too early in the day if the killer was sticking with the timeline she’d put together.

"The medical examiner said the victims are killed on site, so if we get there and there's nobody, maybe we can catch them before they kill again," Nora suggested.

“Unless the killer meant eleven-thirty last night,” Jason pointed out.

“True. Either way, we should probably go check the place out,” Nora recommended.

“I’ll let Detective Wakefield know. Maybe he can connect with the Tarry Bay police and have them meet us there.”

“Good idea.” Nora stood up. They were getting closer. She could feel it.

CHAPTER TWENTY

Nora and Jason parked towards the road, leaving distance between their unmarked sedan and the empty brewery.

Nestled amidst overgrown weeds and crumbling brick walls, the abandoned Batch Brewery stood silent and undisturbed on the edge of Tarry Bay, a sister city to Twisp Harbor. The large windows that had likely once been filled with light, music, and laughter, now were broken or missing altogether.

Detective Wakefield stood out front with another man, who Nora assumed was likely Sergeant Wallace. He was the officer in charge while their captain was on vacation.

The sergeant looked like he was in his late twenties or early thirties, his face full of an earnest eagerness someone new to the force always had. His uniform was crisp and neat, as if it had been freshly ironed, and his shoes shined like they'd never been worn. He stood in stark contrast to the rumpled mess of Detective Wakefield. Nora had to wonder if this was one of the sergeant's first big cases.

As Nora and Jason approached, she noticed Detective Wakefield looked displeased.

"Is it me, or does he not look happy to see us?" Jason asked before they got within earshot, his tone light.

"It's not you." She smiled.

"Thank you for meeting us, Detective Wakefield. I presume this is Sergeant Wallace?" Jason asked as he held out his hand to the stranger.

"Yes, sir," Sergeant Wallace said, shaking Jason's hand firmly enough for it to whiten briefly.

"I'm Agent Snyder. This is my partner, Agent Price. We appreciate your time," Jason said.

"I had a couple of guys check out the place, but nothing's been moved in this place for ages. There's dust settled everywhere, not a single fleck disturbed," the sergeant explained.

"Mind if we take a look around?" Nora asked the two men.

"Not at all. Just don't touch anything," Detective Wakefield warned, completely serious.

Nora nodded, knowing her natural response to scoff at this man wasn't appropriate, especially after the debacle of the night before.

As they entered the brewery, Nora noticed bits of what once was still remained. The copper tanks stood tarnished and empty, grime coating their surfaces from lack of use and upkeep. Hoses laid limp and lifeless, strewn about like forgotten toys, while rusted pipes snaked across the walls.

The sergeant was right. Nothing and no one had been inside this building in months.

"So, right place, wrong time, or wrong place?" Jason asked, just loud enough for Nora to hear.

"Your guess is as good as mine," she sighed.

Every time they seemed to get a lead, it was nothing more than a brutal dead end, the kind that was the road suddenly ending at the edge of a cliff with no warning signs. Frustration was mounting all around, especially by the looks of Detective Wakefield. Nora looked at Jason, fresh out of ideas of what they should do at this point. Wait, and hope the killer had chosen this place for his next murder, or go back to the drawing board?

"Based on the previous timelines and evidence, this killer is likely to strike this evening between eleven and midnight. Can we put some black and whites out here to watch the place?" Jason requested his tone back to its usual polite and respectful cadence.

Nora knew the stakeout was futile, but she'd rather be safe than sorry. The evidence showed the killer was more methodical, a planner. The obelisk was too heavy to maneuver along with a body, so she believed he was setting up at least part of the scene before he brought his victims to their final resting places. She could be wrong, but something in her gut told her she was on the right path.

"We need to look at this from another angle," Nora suggested as they walked back to their vehicle.

"Okay. What do you think we're missing?" Jason asked as he opened her door for her.

"I'm not sure, but there has to be *something*. There always is," she said with a shrug.

Nora climbed into the passenger seat as Jason got behind the wheel.

"Back to the Sheriff's Office?" he asked as he started the car.

“Can we get some food first? I’m starving,” she pleaded, their roles reversed for once.

“That’s a first,” he laughed with a nod.

They agreed to stop for a late lunch at Doyle’s Diner since the sandwiches they’d had were so good. Plus, it had give them space away from the prying eyes of the Newell Sheriff’s Office to discuss the case, brainstorm what else they weren’t seeing.

Jason parked along the street in front of the diner, just a few blocks away from the sheriff’s office. The autumn chill was beginning to infiltrate the days earlier and earlier, something Nora was always surprised by and ill-prepared for. She shivered as an icy wind blew across the side of the building.

“Have you pulled out your fall clothes yet?” Jason asked, holding the glass door to Doyle’s open for her. Nora just shook her head.

“Sit anywhere you want,” someone shouted from the back of the restaurant.

Red vinyl booths lined the counter, each one worn smooth by countless patrons. The chrome stools gleamed, reflecting the lights hanging above, while a jukebox in the corner played a tune Nora didn’t recognize.

Behind the counter, a grizzled cook with a salt-and-pepper goatee worked under fluorescent lights, the sounds of metal scraping metal as he cooked up order after order. Two waitresses, agile and efficient, navigated the floor like veteran dancers, balancing trays laden with hot, steaming plates and empty coffee mugs. The two women, who looked to be in their late forties, hurried about to ensure every customer was tended to.

Laughter and conversation flowed freely from the handful of tables filled with people, all eager to have their appetites satisfied just like Nora and Jason. The clinking of silverware and glasses punctuated the periodic crescendo that ebbed and flowed around them as they located a booth near the back where they could talk in private.

“What can I get you two?” one of the waitresses asked right as they sat down.

“Two coffees and a couple of ice waters please,” Jason answered, their standing drink order pretty much anywhere they went.

“All right, I’ll be right back, Hun,” she said with a cheeky wink and a quick smile.

Nora started to say something, but Jason shook his head before she could get the words out. She looked at the menu and decided a cheeseburger sounded perfect.

The woman returned with their drinks and set them down with ease, careful not to spill them.

"You better keep your distance after that Tuna Melt," Nora warned with a smile after they'd placed their orders.

"Oh no. I'm going to breathe all over you and use every word I can that starts with the letter 'H'," he teased.

"Does this case seem like it's more... challenging... than some of our other cases?" Nora asked, not wanting to dive into anything heavy about the case until they had some food in their bellies to fuel their brains.

"I don't know. I think one of the appealing and also exasperating aspects of this job is that typically no two cases are alike. If they are, then they're probably somehow related," Jason surmised.

"So, kind of like the happy families quote," Nora said.

"The happy families quote?" Jason asked, not following her.

"Yeah, you know the one. *'All happy families are alike; each unhappy family is unhappy in its own way.'* Or something like that. It's from *Anna Karenina*," Nora said, surprised she remembered it as well as she did.

"Ah, I'm not as up on my Russian authors these days as you are apparently," he joked. Then, he added, "But yeah, something like that."

The waitress returned with two hot plates and placed them in front of Nora and Jason.

"Thanks," Nora said with a warm smile.

Nora's stomach gurgled with anticipation as the savory, slightly charred aroma of the cheeseburger wafted up to her nostrils. She realized they hadn't eaten a real meal since probably the leftover pizza and breadsticks the day before.

"This is delicious," Jason said, chewing a large bite of his sandwich.

Nora bit a large chunk out of her burger and nodded in agreement. She had to remind herself to slow down and not eat too fast, knowing she'd have horrible indigestion if she didn't. It was a struggle, though, given how ravenous she was.

"This is why I'm always asking to get food," Jason said as he finished off his Tuna Melt.

"Why?" Nora asked, puzzled by his comment.

"Because if I don't keep food at the forefront, we skip meals and then we end up in fights," Jason smiled, picking up a handful of fries.

"Is that so?" she asked, rolling her eyes with a soft giggle.

"Now that my stomach is satiated, my brain has rebooted and we can discuss the case more adeptly," he announced after he finished off the rest of his fries.

"Same."

"So, what are you thinking, Price?" he asked, leaning back in the booth.

"We're missing something with the victimology," she said, certainty in her voice.

"The only overlap we found was Leon Prescott, and Royce Kimball didn't know him. I checked," Jason pointed out.

"Okay, well we look again. There's something about them that makes this suspect choose them. Something they all have in common," she persisted.

"Like what?" he challenged her.

She knew he'd read the same files she had, so if he wasn't seeing it, maybe she was reaching. But she didn't think she was. There was something there. She could feel it.

"I don't know, but I'm going to find out," she promised.

"Then we should probably head back so you can make your great discovery," Jason suggested.

Nora nodded with a smirk. She took a sip of water as Jason grabbed the ticket the waitress left when she dropped off their food and went to the counter to pay. She knew he was just teasing, but she also knew she was on to something. She could sense it, just like she could sense it was about to snow before it actually did.

"Meet you in the car," Nora called to Jason as he checked out. He nodded and tossed her the keys.

She hurried out the door and to the car, but the icy wind blew past her before she could get the door unlocked. Once inside, she put the keys in the ignition and cranked the vehicle, shivering from the bitter cold. She grabbed Jason's bomber jacket from the backseat and draped it over her. Nora's jacket was back at the station, which didn't do her a lick of good now.

Nora found herself wondering about the victims. What made the killer choose them? There weren't any obvious connections, which meant the killer knew them somehow, or at least knew things about them that weren't public knowledge.

Lynna McLean was single and in her twenties. Boyd Ewen was a military retiree in his second career with a family. His wife hadn't said anything about any financial troubles or health issues. They'd both had some connection – one more than the other – with Leon Prescott, but that hadn't yielded any real leads and their third victim, Royce Kimball, had no link connection whatsoever.

Nora realized as Jason got into the car there was something that linked the three victims.

"I think I have a place to start," she announced. Then, before he could respond, "All of the victims had a connection to legal stuff, and two of them – Lynna and Royce – had had some sort of brush with death before this. Maybe Boyd did, too. Come on. We need to check it out."

CHAPTER TWENTY ONE

Jason poured through all the information he could find on the three victims. He was hoping he could make some kind of over-arching connection with the legal angle. So far, there wasn't anything tangible.

Lynna McLean had been involved with the legal proceedings against Gary Barker, but otherwise, she'd never even had a speeding ticket. Boyd Ewen was a hired consultant in several fraud cases, and he'd been involved as a witness in three trials during his military career. Jason checked out the law firms, the lawyers, the paralegals, anyone connected to the different cases, but again nothing synced between the two victims.

Royce Kimball had been involved in a lawsuit against an apartment complex and another defendant, but it was a civil case. Boyd Ewen and Lynna McLean's cases were all criminal in nature.

Jason sighed loudly, discouraged another angle had turned out to be no lead at all. He looked over at Nora, who's head was buried in her laptop screen. He wondered if she was running into the same dead ends.

"Find anything yet?" he asked Nora, hoping she'd been more fortunate in her search.

"Maybe," she said, sounding distracted.

"Really?" he asked, surprised. He hesitated to feel hopeful, having experienced too many letdowns on this case alone to risk it.

"Maybe," she repeated, her tone a warning to give her space to follow whatever lead she might have.

After their recent squabble, Jason wasn't going to push Nora to do anything she wasn't ready to do. He hated fighting with her, and he didn't want to kick up any dust after it finally seemed like it was settling down. Besides, while Nora could be impulsive about some things, she wasn't impulsive about evidence or leads.

Jason knew Nora tried to keep her assumptions to a minimum when it came to solving cases. If she thought it would help them gain some traction, she'd spitball with him from time-to-time. But mostly she wanted facts, evidence that would hold up in court. It wasn't good enough for her to just solve the case. She wanted to be sure they caught the right person who had be punished accordingly.

When they'd been at the Academy, Nora used to talk about evidence like it was individual threads that made up the fabric of a crime. All it took was finding the right thread to unravel the mystery and solve the case.

Jason had always liked her thread analogy, especially when he thought about how it applied to Nora and her sister's abduction. It helped him understand her and her experience better. Because at the end of the day, Nora knew the right thread was somewhere in her memory bank, locked away behind a vault she didn't know how to open.

Time had become her enemy, rather than her ally. And he knew she struggled with the fact that no matter how hard she'd tried for more than a decade to find Sophia and whoever had taken them, it was her own mind that kept her from pulling apart the tapestry of what had happened to her and her sister.

No matter how much he knew and understood in theory about Nora, he had never experienced anything like what she'd been through. And even if something similar happened to him now, he was much older and had more tools to deal with it than she did at fourteen. Jason recognized that he would never fully comprehend what had happened to her. But it didn't stop him from trying to every day, longing to somehow help make the impossible easier for her.

"They all survived near-death experiences," she said abruptly, interrupting his train of thought.

"What?" Jason asked, perplexed.

"Lynna McLean was shot. She flatlined during surgery, but in the end, she pulled through. Boyd Ewen had had a severe heart attack – something apparently called the 'widow maker' – but he eventually recovered. That's why he retired from the military when he did. And Royce Kimball was almost burned alive in a fire at his apartment building. But he made it. They all survived incidents in which they should have died."

"Okay..." Jason hesitated. He wasn't sure how near-death experiences connected the victims to each other or the killer, other than the fact they'd all had one. Maybe that wasn't as unusual as it seemed. When Nora didn't elaborate, he asked, "So how does that help us?"

"Well, it helps us because all three victims were treated at Newell MultiCare," she explained.

"Okay, that's something. Have you found anything out about who treated them? Maybe the same nurse or doctor?" he asked, his excitement building.

"I'm chatting with the hospital records admin now. He's confirming the doctor on call when the three victims were brought in. It looks like they were treated in the emergency room initially, so they're checking the staff that was on whenever each victim was brought in as well as anyone who might have performed any surgical procedures on them."

Jason hated when their cases hinged on other people getting back to them. It seemed like they were always waiting on someone else to tell them something, which seemed to bring everything to a standstill. If it was up to him, they'd already be in the car headed over to the hospital to figure out who they needed to question first.

"Okay, it looks like they were all treated by the same ER doctor, a Dr. Alpheus Menard. He's been an ER surgeon for a little over a year now. And the staff just confirmed Dr. Menard is on shift for another thirty minutes, and then he's off for the next three days."

Jason checked the time. It was getting late. If Dr. Menard was the killer, he could already have his victim in place. For all they knew, he could have already murdered their fourth victim. The time they were estimating to be the next time of death could be completely wrong and already happened.

"I guess we better skedaddle over to the hospital, then," he suggested.

"Yeah. *Now*," Nora said, breaking into a jog.

CHAPTER TWENTY TWO

Tucked in the center of an office park at the edge of town, Newell MultiCare stood out with its whitewashed façade against the red-bricked buildings around it. It was only two stories, but it spread out like open arms, as if it were embracing the community. Nora was certain the architects had made it that way on purpose.

Nora parked the car in the parking lot marked for emergency room guests, which sat off to the right of the building. The actual emergency room, though, was more centrally located around the back of the building. Thankfully, Nora had grabbed her bomber jacket, so the trek to the ER wasn't too bad in the chilly evening air.

They walked through sliding double doors, their noses immediately pummeled by the smell of lemon-scented antiseptic. The fluorescent lights cast a stark, clinical glow over the waiting room. A low hum of conversation filled the air, punctuated by the occasional cough or sniffle. Rows of plastic chairs, worn and slightly stained, were arranged in a grid, creating a sense of order and security that likely did not continue past the locked double doors where patients were actually being treated.

On the walls, faded posters advertised health services and community events, their colors dulled by time and exposure. A large television mounted in the corner flickered silently, displaying news headlines that scrolled by unnoticed. The air hung heavy with a mixture of antiseptic and anxiety, a potent reminder of the reason everyone was present.

At the center of the room, a harried receptionist worked diligently at a cluttered desk, a wall of Plexi-glass separating her from patients as she juggled phone calls and inquiries. Her face, though tired, displayed a practiced smile and unwavering professionalism. She was the gatekeeper, the first line of defense in this whirlwind of need and urgency.

Scattered throughout the room, patients and their families sat in various states of distress. Some were stoic, their expressions tight with controlled worry. Others fidgeted nervously, their hands wringing together or their eyes glued to the clock above the door.

Nora and Jason held up their credentials as they approached the receptionist.

"Hi there. We need to speak with one of your ER doctors about an ongoing investigation," Jason said, his tone official.

"Okay, I'll have security take you back," she said, waving them towards the locked double doors.

She pressed a button, which opened the doors automatically as she called for a security escort to meet them.

"That was easier than expected," Nora commented quietly, leaning in so no one – including the receptionist – would hear them.

A uniformed officer appeared as they walked through the double door opening.

"Who are you looking for?" the security guard asked, getting right down to brass tacks.

"Dr. Alpheus Menard," Nora said.

"Right this way," he said, turning back towards where he'd come from. They followed behind him as he walked down a sterile, crisp white hallway, large enough to fit two or three gurneys side-by-side.

The hallway bent to the right, opening up to a large room filled with cordoned off curtain-covered rooms and frenetic energy. A cacophony of sounds filled the space, creating a jarring symphony of beeping machines, muffled cries, urgent calls, and the rhythmic whoosh of ventilators.

The fluorescent lights, harsh and unforgiving, illuminated a scene of controlled chaos. Doctors and nurses in crisp white coats moved with swift purpose, their faces etched with a mixture of determination and exhaustion. Each step was calculated, each action precise, as they worked tirelessly to address a multitude of urgent needs.

At the central nurses' station, a flurry of activity unfolded. Charts were scribbled on, phone calls were exchanged, and orders were barked out in rapid succession. The team worked in perfect synchronization, a well-oiled machine fueled by adrenaline and expertise.

"That's Dr. Alfie," the security guard said, pointing at the doctor barking orders to the staff.

Dr. Alpheus Menard glided from the nurses' station to patients smoothly, his white coat billowing behind him. His dark hair, meticulously cut and styled, framed the sharp angles of his face in a way that made him seem more approachable. He moved about with a confident gait, commanding the room seamlessly as he moved from one patient to the next.

"Dr. Menard?" Jason called out, catching the doctor mid-stride.

"What are you doing in my ER?" the doctor demanded.

"We need to speak with you somewhere privately, please," Jason insisted.

Nora and Jason both held up their FBI badges before he could respond.

"Do you not see I'm in the middle of treating *all* of these patients?" he snapped.

"Dr. Menard, it's imperative we speak with you immediately. We can do so here, which means you'll get back to your patients faster, or we can put you in handcuffs and perp walk you out of here," Nora threatened.

The doctor's eyes darkened with anger, like a dangerous storm brewing off the coast.

"Come with me," he barked, acquiescing.

Dr. Menard quickly led them out of the patient triage area, down a different hallway than the one they'd come in from, and into a small waiting room with a loveseat and two chairs.

Nora noticed a sign posted to the right of the door frame of the room they were walking into. *Family Consultation Room.* This had to be where they took people to tell them bad news. She wondered how many tears had been shed inside it.

"You have two minutes," the doctor declared, not waiting for them to sit.

"We have as much time as we need, Dr. Menard," Jason corrected.

The doctor sighed loudly, his irritation at their interruption coloring his every word and movement. He sat down in one of the chairs across from Nora and Jason and stared at them expectantly.

"There have been three murders in the last week in and around Newell. After some investigation, we've found you have treated each of the victims in the past. We would like to discuss those patients with you," Jason explained, careful with his words.

Nora was glad Jason was the one explaining the situation. She knew it was a delicate balance when it came questioning a suspect and keeping them in the dark for as long as possible that they might be a person of interest in the case. She didn't want to ruin their chances of catching the doctor off guard because she'd said too much upfront.

In the five years they'd been partners, Jason had always led the way, with her quickly chiming in afterwards.

"Do you have a warrant?" the doctor asked, crossing his arms in front of him, creating a barrier.

"Do we need one?" Nora challenged.

"Do I need a lawyer," Dr. Menard countered.

"Are you a murderer?" Jason asked boldly.

Nora glanced at him in surprise.

"What? No!" the doctor shouted.

"Then you don't need a lawyer," Jason reasoned.

"What do you want to know?" the doctor capitulated, waving a figurative white flag.

"You treated Lynna McLean for a gunshot wound, Boyd Ewen for a heart attack, and Royce Kimball for burns within the last year. Do you remember them?" Nora asked as Jason pulled out his notebook to capture any pertinent information.

"Of course I do. I treated them, and they went home. Why?" the doctor asked, his contempt resurfacing.

"Because someone killed them and you're the only one who knew all three," Nora said, her tone as sharp and precise as a scalpel.

"Wait just a minute. You cannot possibly think I killed people I treated, that I helped? You're not that desperate, are you?" Dr. Menard accused.

"We're following the evidence," Jason responded.

"I don't kill people. It's part of the whole Hippocratic Oath. Maybe you should read it," the doctor suggested, his words dripping in sarcasm.

"Good. You'll have no problem providing an alibi for the three deaths, then," Nora shrugged nonchalantly.

"This is ridiculous! I literally save lives all day long, including the three people you just mentioned. And one of them, I not only saved once, but twice! Why would I kill them?" the doctor screeched, his mask of composure slipping.

Nora looked at Jason.

Twice?

"Who did you save twice?" he asked, picking up on the same thread.

"Boyd Ewen."

"How?" Nora interjected, curious to know more.

"After he retired from the Air Force, he took a factory job to keep busy. There was some accident with one of the machines, and he was brought in with a severed femoral artery and no pulse. I stopped the bleeding, pounded on his chest until his heart started again, and gave him a blood transfusion. He walked out of here less than a week later. Then, last year, he came in with a numb left arm and jaw pain. I tested his enzymes, and he was in the throes of a myocardial infarction. I got him into surgery to put some stints in, but he flatlined on my table. I pulled out every trick in my book to get that man's heart to start beating, and after two minutes, it did," the doctor recounted.

There was an element of pride in the way he described how he'd helped Boyd Ewen, like he'd taken on God and won. Not once, but twice.

Nora looked at Jason and then back at Dr. Menard. He wasn't their killer. But he might be the reason the killer is murdering people.

"Thank you for your cooperation, Dr. Menard. We'll contact you if we have any other questions," Nora said matter-of-factly, dismissing the doctor from their pseudo-interrogation.

The doctor stood up and let out a heavy sigh. Then, he looked at the two of them. For the first time since they encountered the doctor, Nora noticed how weary his eyes looked.

"I'm sorry someone took my patients' lives. I tried to give them something more, a chance to do more with the time they almost lost. They didn't deserve to have that taken away, and I genuinely hope you catch whoever did this," the doctor said, his voice gentle and full of concern.

"Thank you, Dr. Menard," Jason nodded.

The doctor nodded in return without another word, and left Nora and Jason in the Family Consultation Room.

Nora checked the time on her phone. It was getting late, but she knew she needed to get in touch with Libby Cates. She pulled up the woman's contact information from the case file in her email and dialed the number.

"Hi, Ms. Cates? This is Agent Price with the FBI. Yes, I know. I'm sorry for calling so late. Something has come up, and I was hoping you could help. Before the bodega shooting, had Lynna ever had a near-death experience?" Nora asked, doing her best not to sound overly hopeful.

Jason looked over at Nora, his brows furrowing over his blue eyes in curiosity.

"Near-death experience?" the woman asked, confused.

"Yes, did she almost die in an accident or something before the shooting?" Nora clarified.

"No, nothing like that. She had Leukemia as a child, but it was treatable."

"Did Lynna have any complications with her treatment?" Nora asked, worried the thread they'd found was disintegrating before they'd even gotten to pull on it.

"Well, let me think. It was ages ago, but I think I remember Mama saying she'd had some kind of reaction to the drugs they gave her. Yes, now that I think about it. She went into anaphylactic shock. Scared my parents to death."

"Thank you so much, Ms. Cates. That's what we needed to know. We'll call you when we have more to discuss," Nora said.

"All right. Thank you, Agent Price," the woman said politely before ending the call.

"You going to fill me in, partner?" Jason asked eagerly.

"Just a second," she said, holding up her index finger.

Nora pulled up Royce Kimball's file on her phone and quickly scanned it. She was fairly certain she'd seen something in the medical examiner's report about scarred lungs or something. As she scrolled through, she found the comment.

"Scar tissues in the lungs from previous drowning," she read aloud.

"Wait. What?"

"The victims didn't just cheat death once, Jason. They all almost died *twice*. The whole makeshift sundial thing? That's the killer saying their time is up," Nora explained, her adrenaline surging now that they finally had something solid to go on.

"So, we have our motive," Jason sighed with relief. "Even if it doesn't make a whole lot of sense to anyone sane."

"Yep, and now we have a way to possibly find his next target. The downside, though, is we're running out of time."

CHAPTER TWENTY THREE

The man stared at the picture of his sister, Aline, on his computer screen. She'd been so vibrant, so full of life, and then suddenly she was gone. His boss had tried to tell him he could take as much time as he needed, but it hadn't been good for Austen to be idle. He was so angry all the time. He could not just sit around crying all day.

Aline was seventeen months younger than him. She was everything he could have wished for in a sister, so warm and kindhearted, a walking ray of sunshine. They group up in a tight-knit family, especially because they were so close in age. They'd done everything together, as kids and then as adults. Aline wasn't just his sister, she was also his best friend, a forever constant in his life.

That all changed three weeks ago.

Aline had been driving home one evening from visiting their parents in Boston when she saw a vehicle stranded on the side of the road with its hazard lights on. A woman was trying to change one of the back tires, and no one had stopped to help. Aline turned off on the next exit and came back around to make sure the woman was okay.

Aline pulled up behind the car, leaving her lights on. It was getting dark, and she was worried the woman was having a hard time because she could not see what she was doing. She'd texted him, letting him know she was running late because she'd stopped to help someone. He immediately asked her to stay in her car and call for help. She never replied.

He later learned that as Aline approached the woman, a pickup truck traveling at high speed lost control and veered off the road. The truck careened into Aline's car, the sheer impact forcing her parked car forward and crushing Aline between the woman's car and her own. His sister had died instantly. There was no resuscitation, no near-death experiences. She was just gone.

His parents had tried to pass it off as a tragic accident, like it was just something he should accept. But he could not. He knew miracles happened. He saw remnants of them all the time at work. He'd worked for Newell MultiCare as a medical billing specialist for ten years. He knew the codes frontwards and backwards, and there were instances almost daily of people dying and being brought back to life thanks to the life-saving measures doctors and paramedics had taken. He and his coworker, Gabe, had nicknamed the codes the Resurrection Codes.

He just didn't understand why Aline could not have been one of those miracles. If anyone deserved to come back to life, it was his sister. The more he thought about how unfair it all was, the more he realized these people who were being saved were nothing more than common thieves. They'd stolen time from other people, people like his sister, who should still be alive and well right now.

He'd tried to move on, tried to work through his anger. And then, he started to notice something that he could not ignore. There were people like Lynna McLean who had miraculously survived a near-death experience not once but twice. They were thieves of the worst kind – greedy and selfish people who didn't deserve another second breathing stolen air.

A week ago, Lynna McLean had been brought into the emergency room by her sister. She thought she was having a heart attack or something. It turned out the woman was just having a panic attack and was sent home with some anti-anxiety medication. When her file came across his desk, he recognized her name, but he wasn't sure why. He accessed her records and realized who she was.

Lynna McLean had survived a fatal gunshot wound a year ago. And decades before that, she'd survived some kind of fatal allergic reaction to her chemotherapy drugs. Unbridled rage overwhelmed him as he read each word telling him this woman had been brought back to life on two different occasions. She'd stolen time from others for *years*. It was the most egregious offense he could imagine, especially after losing Aline so recently.

The man never intended on becoming a killer. At first, he thought someone like Lynna McLean was just a one-off, a true miracle. Then, he found Boyd Ewen's file. And Royce Kimball. They weren't miracles. They were crooks, and they didn't deserve to live another minute as far as he was concerned.

When he killed Lynna McLean, he watched the stolen time seep from her eyes, and he knew at that moment he could not stop. He would not. He had to keep the balance and stop these horrible people from living lives that weren't theirs.

He pulled up the file on the woman he'd found who had stolen more than any of the others. She'd died twice, and she'd killed someone. She was the worst he'd come across so far, and he'd known as soon as he'd come across her records that she was the next one who had to go.

He closed out the files, cleared his cache and browsing history, and logged off for the day. The woman was likely out with friends still, about to stumble home to her apartment where he'd be waiting. He watched his sister's face disappear from the computer screen almost as quickly as it had in real life. The pain clutched its jagged claws around his heart at the thought, and he knew the only way it would stop was when he watched the woman take her last stolen breath.

CHAPTER TWENTY FOUR

Nora and Jason hurried back to the emergency room, hoping Dr. Menard could connect them with someone in the records department.

"What now?" the doctor shouted at them as soon as he saw them.

"We need to talk to someone who has access to hospital records. You helped us figure out how the killer's finding his victims," Nora explained.

"Now I know you need a warrant for *that*," Dr. Menard challenged.

"Doctor, call the hospital lawyers or whoever you have to, but this is an emergency. The suspect is targeting people who had at least two near-death experiences. They are finding these people using your hospital system's medical records, and they are going to strike again tonight. We need your help," Nora begged, desperate for the doctor to understand how serious this was.

"I'll take you to see Jean Chapman. She's in charge of hospital records," the doctor offered.

"Thank you so much," Nora sighed, relieved he was helping them.

The doctor led them through the maze of hospital hallways until they reached an open door with a sign hanging above it that said 'Records'.

"Hi, Ms. Chapman. This is Agent Price and Agent Snyder with the FBI. They need help, and I know you're the only person in this entire place who might be able to assist them," the doctor said, laying the flattery on thick. Then, Dr. Menard left them in the woman's charge.

Jean Chapman was a petite, compact woman with a smooth, round face. Her dark curly hair was piled into a messy bun on top of her head, her small bright blue eyes scrutinizing every inch of the two FBI agents in front of her.

"Credentials please," she requested, immediately holding out her hand, before they could explain what they needed.

Nora and Jason immediately pulled out their badges and handed them to her. She looked at each badge and returned them.

"How can I help you, Agents?"

"We're investigating three murders in the area, and the suspect is targeting people who have nearly died at least twice. We know, without any doubt, the suspect already had their target and is going to kill them tonight. What we don't know is who their target is," Nora explained, hoping she was making sense.

"Okay, but I can't just search for patients who 'nearly died at least twice'. What other search criteria do you have?" the woman asked.

Jean Chapman looked at Nora and Jason like they were two complete idiots, and Nora could not help but wonder if she was right to do so. They didn't have any specific criteria. The victims were all different ages, different genders, and from different socio-economic backgrounds.

"We believe the killer has access to your hospital system records. Besides you, who all has that kind of access?" Jason questioned.

"The medical billing specialists, the insurance folks, most of the medical staff, pretty much anyone with a system login.

"Okay, that sounds like a lot of people," Nora said.

"At least a thousand," the woman nodded in agreement.

"Excuse us one second, please," Jason said, pulling Nora aside for a private chat.

"There's got to be another way to do this. We're wasting time we don't have," he whispered, trying to keep the woman from overhearing them.

"Right. So, what do we know for sure about this killer?" Nora countered, keeping her voice low.

"White, early-to-mid forties, single. Most likely a male, given the strength it would take to move the bodies and the obelisks. He likely lives alone, but he might have recently moved back home. The murders are part of some larger vendetta, so maybe he lost someone recently," Jason rattled off.

"Exactly. And he has access to the records, which means he's likely an employee," Nora pointed out.

Jason nodded and stepped back into Jean Chapman's office.

"We're looking for a white male, early forties, who recently lost someone important to him that has access to patient medical files. Anyone like that ring a bell?" Nora asked, hoping something would shake loose.

“No, but if he has access to the files, we can find him by pulling up the files he accessed,” Jean Chapman said with a smile, like she’d just solved their case for them.

“What do you mean?” Jason asked, his curiosity piqued.

“Digital records have a history of access, kind of like a digital fingerprint. If you know whose records this person accessed, I can pull them up and check the access logs,” she explained.

“Perfect!” Jason shouted excitedly.

“Hand me your notebook,” Nora directed. Jason did as he was told, and she quickly scribbled down the three names of the victims. Then, she tore the paper from the notebook and handed it over to Jean Chapman.

“We need to know who accessed all three of the patients’ records in the last month. Can you do that?” Nora asked, hoping the answer was a resounding ‘yes’.

“Give me two shakes of a lambs’ tail and I’ll give you a name,” the woman promised.

Nora and Jason watched as the woman began typing and clicking furiously like she was some sort of hacker genius. They could see in the reflection of her too-large, framed glasses she was clicking through dozens of screens, running searches as she went.

Maybe she was a hacker in a past life, Nora thought to herself.

“Got it. Austen Darby is the only person who’s accessed all three patient records. He’s a medical billing specialist, so the system didn’t flag him for unauthorized access, or I would’ve found him sooner,” the woman said, shaking her head.

“Okay, great. Great job. Um. Are there any records Austen Darby accessed in the past couple of days that stand out?” Nora inquired.

They now had the killer’s name, but she wanted to make sure they knew who he was going after.

“It looks like he’s been working the last couple of days, so let me see if I can filter out anyone who had a recent medical issue. Only one of the three previous victims had been in recently, and none of them had outstanding balances, so the system should have flagged at lcast two of those accounts for unauthorized access, even for a billing specialist,” the woman explained as she typed away, continuing her search.

“I can wait here while she pulls up the information if you want to go get the car and call in an APB for Austen Darby,” Nora offered.

“Okay. Ms. Chapman, where’s the nearest exit?” Jason asked, interrupting her search.

“Look to your left. See the exit sign at the end of the hallway? That’ll take you out to the outpatient parking lot,” she smirked, peering over her glasses like she was a teacher scolding a student for asking her a dumb question.

“Thank you,” Jason grumbled and took off down the hallway.

“Sorry, it’s gonna take a minute. This guy’s an efficient billing specialist,” she stated, her tone appreciative of Austen Darby’s effectiveness as an employee.

“Yeah, he’s a pretty efficient killer, too,” Nora snapped, irritated at the woman’s insensitivity.

“Jeez, sorry. I just... never mind,” the woman shook her head, her cheeks reddening.

“No, I’m sorry. I didn’t mean to be rude,” Nora apologized.

She checked her phone. They were cutting it too close. Hopefully, Jason had gotten to the car by now and called in the guy’s information to dispatch.

“Yahtzee! You’re looking for Veda Layton,” Jean Chapman declared. She quickly wrote the name on the back of the paper Nora had given her earlier and handed it back to Nora.

“Thank you so much, Ms. Chapman,” Nora smiled, grateful and relieved they finally had something concrete.

Nora hurried down the hallway to the exit, texting the woman’s name Jean Chapman had given her to Jason and Detective Wakefield. They knew who the killer was, who he was likely going to kill, and what time it was going to happen. They just weren’t one hundred percent sure where he was going to do it.

As Nora burst through the exit door into the cool night air, she could not help but feel some relief at the sight of Jason sitting in the car waiting for her. Maybe, just maybe, if they had a little bit of luck on their side, they’d stop Austen Darby from taking a fourth life.

CHAPTER TWENTY FIVE

"I don't think he's going to take her to Batch Brewery. Do you remember any of the other locations on your list?" Nora prodded as she got in the car.

"I'm not sure, but we can check. Dispatch put out an APB on both Austen Darby and Veda Layton. Maybe someone will spot one or both of them before he can get to her," Jason sighed.

"Hopefully," Nora said, trying to stay optimistic.

"Wakefield emailed us a list of abandoned buildings in the area. Veda Layton lives in Carson, so that could be a potential angle," Jason said, filling her in on the additional goings-on she'd missed.

Nora pulled up her email and read through Detective Wakefield's email. There was only one possible building in Carson that fit Austen Darby's M.O.

"I think he's taking her to the Carson Culinary Warehouse. It's been abandoned for about a year, and it was financed through Newell Savings and Loan. According to the maps app, it's about ten minutes away," Nora directed.

"I'm sure we can get there quicker than that," Jason smiled, his daredevil showing.

Nora radioed Dispatch and provided the address to the Carson Culinary Warehouse, requesting backup. This time, she was bringing the calvary with her.

She looked at her phone and realized they were out of time. "Jason, hurry!" she urged, eager to stop Austen Darby before he could kill again.

Jason pressed the gas to the floor, making the car lunge forward faster than ever. Nora braced herself, gripping the dashboard and side of the door. She had no doubt that Jason would get them there in one piece. She just hated feeling out of control.

They were going so fast, Jason almost missed the half-bent sign by the highway, causing him to yank the wheel hard to the right. Nora felt her stomach pitch with the motion of the car. She'd never been more grateful in her life that she hadn't had anything to eat recently.

Jason slowed down and turned off his lights as they pulled up to the warehouse. The building emerged from the ground like a large gravestone against the night sky, an image Nora could have done without in her mind.

"Where is everybody?" Nora asked as Jason parked and turned the engine off.

"On the way, hopefully," Jason responded.

Nora worried they were too late. She carefully opened the car door and listened for any sounds of movement around them. At first, she could only hear the constant, rhythmic buzzing sound of crickets. Then, she heard a door close from somewhere near the back side of the building.

"I'll go around back, you come in the front, and hopefully we'll meet in the middle," she whispered. Then, she quietly closed her door and took off towards the warehouse.

"Nora," Jason hissed in the darkness, calling after her as inaudibly as possible. Nora heard him, but she didn't stop. She could not. Austen Darby was not going to claim another victim if she could help it.

Nora gently pulled her gun from the holster on her side and clicked the safety off, doing her best to be as silent as possible. She aimed it in front of her as she approached a darkened opening that likely used to be a door. She stopped and listened to make sure there wasn't someone just beyond the doorframe, waiting to jump her.

When she didn't hear anything but the sounds of her own breathing, she stepped into the darkness of the building. As her eyes adjusted, she realized it wasn't as dark inside the warehouse as it had seemed.

Dark, twisted steel beams jutted from the ceiling, their rust-colored tears staining the concrete floor. Amidst the debris and decay, remnants of the warehouse's former life lay scattered like discarded relics. Empty crates huddled together, their faded logos unreadable without more light. Old machinery and conveyor belts lingered mostly in the shadows, as if they were waiting to be reclaimed.

Nora progressed towards the center of the warehouse as planned, but she didn't hear anything that would indicate Austen Darby was on the premises. She started to call out to Jason when a light suddenly turned on with a click in the left corner closest to her. Nora immediately crouched to the ground by the empty crates.

"Wake up, thief!" an angry voice snarled, visceral hate emanating from every syllable. The voice was coming from the same direction as the light. Then, she heard a rough, grinding scrape across the floor.

He must be moving the obelisk.

Nora charged towards the sound and light, her gun aimed and ready to fire.

“FBI! Freeze!” she shouted as the scene came into full view.

Austen Darby whirled around to face her, fury filling his ragged face.

“You can’t stop me!” he challenged, springing towards Nora with all his might.

Before she could pull the trigger, he’d knocked the gun from her hand and pinned her to the ground.

“Austen Darby, you are under arrest for the murders of Lynna McLean, Boyd Ewen, and Royce Kimball!” she shouted, struggling to free herself from his grip.

Austen leaned over her and looked her straight in the face. “Nice try,” he laughed.

“Get off me,” she shouted at him, kicking and doing her best to try and buck him off of her.

“I’d do what the lady says if I were you,” Jason suggested as he held his pistol to the back of Austen’s head.

Nora exhaled, thankful Jason had stepped in.

“Put your hands up and get off of me right now,” she demanded.

Austen Darby put his hands above his head and slowly lifted himself up and off of Nora. She rolled out from under him and stood up. Jason kept his weapon trained on the suspect as Nora cuffed him. Once he was secured, she rushed over to motionless body by the obelisk.

“Veda? Can you hear me?” Nora called to the woman as she checked her pulse. She quickly untied the ropes Austen had bound her with and continued trying to rouse her.

“Police!” a loud voice shouted as a band of uniformed officers suddenly descended on the scene.

“We need a paramedic,” Nora shouted, struggling to get the woman to wake up. There was some blood on the concrete where her head was, so Nora didn’t dare move her. Like the others, Austen had probably hit her in the back of the head to immobilize her.

"Somebody mirandize this idiot," Jason directed, shoving the handcuffed Austen in to the crowd of officers. They shoved him around as they made their way out of the warehouse, roughing him up just enough to rattle him as they went.

The paramedics arrived in a flurry of movement, scooping Veda Layton off of the floor and disappearing with her as quickly as they'd appeared.

Jason held his hand out to Nora, who was still crouching on the ground next to where Veda had been. She gripped his hand and he pulled her to her feet.

"I think we both need some food, a hot shower, and a good night's rest. What do you think?" he asked with his biggest grin.

"I think Doyle's has a cheeseburger with my name on it," she said.

CHAPTER TWENTY SIX

Nora parked her car in front of her parents' house. She was tired, sore, and so relieved to have some time off. Austen Darby was going to rot in prison for a long time, and Veda Layton walked away with a mild concussion. Nora and Jason had caught creep number thirty-five, which felt like the first good thing that had happened in a while.

Nora had called her mom when she was on her way over, hoping to catch her alone. It was always harder to talk to her mom when he was around. Fortunately, he wasn't home, so Nora hurried to their house as quickly as possible.

When she walked in the door, she knew something wasn't quite right. "Mom?" she called out, the house unusually silent.

"Back here," her mother answered.

Nora walked down the hallway towards her parents' room, but then realized the door to her sister's room was open.

"Hi, Nora," her mother said, confirming in Sophia's room, sitting on her bed.

"Hi, Mom," Nora smiled as she leaned on the doorframe.

Nora hadn't stepped foot in Sophia's room since she disappeared. She hadn't been allowed in Sophia's room when she was home, and as far as Nora was concerned, that was still true. Nora's mom patted the empty space on the bed beside her, as if inviting Nora to join her.

"I'm good," Nora declined.

"I come in here all the time when your dad isn't home. It helps. I don't know why, but I feel closer to her when I sit in here," her mom said quietly, a confession she'd kept to herself for over a decade.

"It's okay to talk about Sophia. I do. I talk about her all the time," Nora shrugged, like it was no big deal. Then, she added, "It's why I started going to group therapy. So I could talk about her."

"I can't go back to that place," Nora's mother said as her face crumpled in her hands. Nora froze. It had been years since she'd seen her mother cry, and she didn't know what to do. Her mother began to sob, years of unresolved guilt and trauma coming to the surface.

"Oh, mom," Nora sighed, forcing herself to go to her mother and comfort her. She hugged her mom tightly, which only made her cry more. "It's also okay to be sad."

Her mom's tears slowed as she sighed deeply and slowly moved out of Nora's embrace. "I just miss her so much. I thought I could be brave like you and go to those sessions, but they just made it worse. And then the whole Trudie thing... what if that's what happens to me?"

"What do you mean?" Nora asked, gently rubbing her mom's back.

"One of the ladies from the group said Trudie killed herself because she'd never gotten over what had happened to her. That she was a 'delayed victim'," her mom explained, using air quotes around the term *delayed victim*.

"You're not Trudie, Mom," Nora reassured her mother.

"No, but I feel all this stuff all the time, and it never goes away. I feel guilty I didn't pick you girls up that day, or that you were even working in that crummy diner to begin with. I won't let your father disconnect our home phone because what if Sophia tries to call? I refuse to move or find somewhere new to live because what if she comes home and we're not here? And honestly, I don't want to be anywhere she hasn't been, and I don't think he understands it," her mom explained, her eyes welling up with tears again, her voice cracking as she uttered Sophia's name.

"This isn't healthy, Mom. You've got to talk to someone who can help you. Otherwise, it's going to eat you alive," Nora warned, genuinely worried for her mother's wellbeing.

"Like who? A therapist?" she asked, woefully looking up at Nora.

"Yeah, someone who deals with grief and loss and stuff like this," Nora recommended with a nod.

"What's going on?" Nora's dad barked, suddenly appearing in the doorway of Sophia's room. Nora jumped up at the sharpness of his tone. She hadn't heard him speak to her like that since before Sophia had gone missing.

"Mom and I were just talking..." Nora started to explain, but he cut her off.

"Get out of this room! Now!" he demanded and turned on his heel, leaving Nora and her mother slack-jawed at the level of rage he'd projected towards them.

Nora jumped up and went after him. "What's so bad about Mom wanting to talk to someone? It has *nothing* to do with you," she shouted after him as he stormed into the living room.

He whirled around, his face so red it was almost purple. "This is *my* house, Nora. You do not get to raise your voice at me in *my* house," he warned.

"This used to be *my* house, too, Dad. Or am I not welcome here now?" she challenged.

"Keep pushing, Nora, and that's exactly what's going to happen," he threatened, his tone becoming more menacing with every retort.

"Dad. Do you hear yourself? You're furious because I was talking to Mom about getting help. She *needs* to talk to someone about what happened to me and Soph...".

"Don't you dare say her name. You don't get to come in here and dredge all that mess up, projecting your guilt and shame and trauma onto us because you don't know how to move on," he roared.

"What are you talking about? *None* of us have moved on, Dad. You're both just faking it until you make it, and it's not working. Can't you see that? Or do you want to bury Mom, too?" Nora snarled back.

For a moment, Nora thought her father might hit her. But he didn't. She could tell he might've thought about it, though.

"Get out and leave us be, Nora. It's enough. We've all had enough of this drama to last us ten lifetimes," he said with bitter resolve.

"Are you serious? You're putting *this* on *me*? I didn't do anything, Dad!" she shrieked, incredulous.

"You're right. You didn't. You just left her, and we've had to live with that for over a decade. Now, get out!" he screamed.

Nora heard her mom gasp from behind her dad. She wanted to run away from this stranger her dad had become and never come back, but her feet were frozen in place. Rage and despair ravaged her insides as the words her father had just shouted at her repeated in her brain over and over.

"Just so you know, every day I wish it had been Sophia who had come home instead of me," she admitted softly for the first time to her parents before she finally forced her body to move. As she turned to leave, she saw the ferocity in her father's face wilt into despair, but it was too late. He'd gone too far.

At the door, she turned back and looked at the people her parents had become, both of them in different stages of the grief process even after all these years. Then, choking back tears, she croaked, “I’m sorry I’m the one who got away.”

CHAPTER TWENTY SEVEN

Nora watched Dane flip through the channels, looking for something they'd both enjoy watching. She liked seeing him in her apartment, sitting on her couch. It felt like it was the start of something more serious, but they hadn't actually had the talk to make it something official.

"So I've been thinking about us a lot lately," Nora said, doing her best to sound casual.

"Oh yeah?" Dane replied, almost absentmindedly.

"Yeah," she nodded.

"Okay..." he said, still flipping through the channels.

Nora looked at him like he had a third eye in the middle of his forehead. "Did you hear what I said?" she asked, fairly confident he hadn't.

"You said you'd been thinking about us," he said with a shrug. Then, he glanced at her and added, "So, what about us have you been thinking about?"

"I don't know. I thought maybe it was time to talk about making this thing between us something official," she sighed, not sure she wanted to pursue the topic any longer.

"Is that something you want?" he asked, briefly looking her way.

"I don't know," she said softly.

"Okay," he replied, much to her annoyance.

Nora let out a long, frustrated sigh. This was not going the way she'd planned. She'd thought about everything he might say, every argument she could make, but lack of interest was not something she'd anticipated.

"Something bothering you?" he asked as he muted the television and put the remote on the coffee table, giving her his full attention.

"You seem distracted lately. Distant. Is something going on?" she asked, her confidence in their connection shrinking.

He looked around, as if the explanation was somewhere hidden in the room. "I've just got a lot on my mind, that's all."

"Look, I like you, Dane. A lot. But I can't commit to someone who won't talk to me and open up about stuff going on in your life," she told him, setting a boundary with him she'd failed to set with her parents.

He nodded slowly. "I promise, it's just something personal and has nothing to do with you. I'm not trying to be secretive or whatever. I just know you have a lot going on, and I don't want to add to your already overflowing plate. Especially not after the thing with your dad," he explained in a calm voice.

Nora bristled at the mention of her father, the wounds still too fresh to think about, much less hear someone reference them.

"Dane..." she started, but she didn't get the chance to refute his reasoning. Her phone buzzed on the side table next to her, interrupting the moment. She glanced at it. Jason.

Picking it up, she said, "Howdy, partner."

"I'm three minutes out. Get dressed and be ready to go when I get there," he directed.

"What? Please don't tell me we got another case already," she whined, mouthing *sorry* to Dane as she got up from the couch.

"Maybe. I was following up on the Samantha Banks' case you'd told me about. You know, keeping my ears open for any chatter, or whatever. And I think I might have something," he said, his voice as serious as she'd ever heard it.

"What do you mean?" she asked, confused. "*You've* been looking into it?"

"Yeah. And listen to this. A girl is missing. They think she's been abducted, like just a few hours ago, not far from here. And Nora, I swear it reads just like you and your sister's abduction," he explained.

"How?" was the only word she could manage, her insides tangling up with fear and adrenaline at the thought they might have a lead and the idea another girl had been taken.

"A young woman, I think her name is Summer, was walking home through the woods when an older man grabbed her."

Nora gasped. "How do you know this?"

"Someone saw it happen," he said.

"Oh my god," she replied, her body going numb.

"And the thing is, Nora, if you're right about the abandoned churches angle, we might be able to find him. But we've got to go as soon as I get there."

"I'm putting my shoes on now and I'll meet you outside," she said, scanning the floor for them.

"Another case?" Dane asked as she hung up the phone.

"Something like that," she said, not wanting to get into it with him. If he was going to keep secrets from her, she was going to do the same.

"I can walk you out," he offered.

"No. I'd rather you not. I'm not ready to get into all that with Jason, so can you just wait until he picks me up please?" she asked, her tone entreating and annoyed at the same time.

"Um, sure. Yeah, no problem." He leaned back on the couch and watched her run around, getting everything together. Then, he added, "I'm sorry we didn't have more time to talk about the whole making it official thing."

"It's fine," she said, giving him a tight smile.

Nora didn't know a lot about Dane, and that seemed to be how he liked it. Maybe he would always be that way. In the back of her mind, she worried she was way more invested in their budding relationship than he was, but right now she had more important things to focus on.

A horn honked twice outside. Jason had arrived.

"Just twist the lock on the door and pull it closed when you leave," she said, swiping her lips lightly across his cheek before she headed for the door.

She had a case to solve, and this time, it might just be her own.

EPILOGUE

Dane sat in his car in the parking lot and started to text Nora, again.

He'd been acting like an ass these past few weeks.

And Nora deserved an explanation. Out of everyone in his life, she was likely the one person who would understand what he was going through the most.

Or maybe . . . maybe it would be too much. Even for her.

So every time typed out a few words, he'd just end up tapping the delete key and swiping out of the messaging app.

Nora didn't need another burden to carry. She'd already been through so much, and now she was working a case that needed her full attention. She had to stay focused on her work, and he hated the idea of dumping his troubles on her when there was nothing she could do to make them better. It was hard enough for him to accept his lack of control in the situation. He didn't need to remind Nora how helpless she could be, too.

Dane had changed his tie six times before he finally picked the first one he'd originally put on. He was so jittery, he could not get his hands to stop shaking as he walked through the blue-grey concrete halls of the Babcock Federal Penitentiary, following a prison guard to the room where the parole board hearing was being held.

Two weeks prior, Dane had received the unwelcome letter informing him his brother's parole eligibility was being reviewed. As far as he'd known, his brother was sentenced to life in prison *without* parole, so this was news to him. It had taken him a full day to track down someone at the District Attorney's office who could tell him what was going on. The prison psychologist working with him requested the hearing, stating there was some additional information that needed to be considered in his case.

It was like a punch in his gut. The one thing that eased his nightmares was the certainty that he'd never see his brother again.

A tense anticipation hung heavy in the air of the sterile parole hearing room as Dane sat patiently waiting for his brother's turn. Sunlight filtered through the barred windows, illuminating the plain, grey-blue walls and the faces of the three parole board members scrutinizing the inmate seated before them.

When the door swung open, Dane bit his tongue. Then, he watched as the guards escorted his older brother in.

John Baxter Reed did not look at him. He walked with his head down, to his chair at the front of the room, and sat ramrod straight, his worn prison uniform a stark contrast to the polished attire of the board members. His brother's face was etched with the lines of weariness and strain from the years he'd spent behind bars.

Dane didn't recognize anything about his brother. He was a stranger and had been for almost two decades. If Dane was honest with himself, his brother had always been a stranger. A violent and dangerous stranger.

The board president, a stern woman with a piercing gaze, began the proceedings. Her voice was devoid of emotion as she recounted his brother's crime, the details echoing in the room like a chilling verdict, a reminder of the life John had taken from Dane. Dane watched his brother as he listened with a bowed head, his shoulders slumping as if the weight of his past was too much to bear.

Dane wanted to believe his brother felt remorse. But he knew better. He'd been there the night he'd killed their parents and had tried to kill Dane. There was no soul in that man's eyes when he was a teenager, and Dane didn't believe he'd grown a conscience as an adult. It just wasn't possible for people like that.

The board president called for a Dr. Garland to come to the front and speak. Dane looked around, wondering who this doctor was and why they felt it so important to try to get his psychopathic brother out of prison.

It was when a dark brunette in a crisp maroon suit stood up and walked confidently in front of the parole board that Dane understood.

He'd heard rumors over the years of how charming his brother was, how he seemed popular with the female prison pen pals. Women always thought they could tame the bad boy. The thought disgusted him too much to find out more. Now, he regretted being so stubborn. Maybe if he had taken the time to find out what was going on at Babcock, he would not be sitting in the parole hearing today.

"Dr. Garland, please provide your name, professional credentials, and relation to the prisoner," the board president instructed.

"Dr. Enid Garland, American Board of Professional Psychology board certified clinical psychologist. I've been treating Mr. Reed for the last three years, pro bono," the woman responded.

"Thank you, Doctor. Please explain your concerns," the president directed.

"I'm here today to provide my expert opinion on the medical care John Baxter Reed needs to address his mental health issues in a productive and rehabilitative way. At sixteen, Mr. Reed murdered his parents in a drug-induced state of paranoia and rage. He attacked his younger brother, who was also in the home, and he left him for dead," the woman said flatly, recounting the most horrific time in Dane's life like it was as simple as a stubbed toe.

Dane listened to what the doctor was saying, unable to process the words. The only word that flooded his mind seemed to block out any other thought: *Monster.*

His brother was a monster.

Dane looked at the parole board members, desperate to believe they weren't seriously considering whatever this crazy woman was recommending. How could they be considering any changes to his prison term if he'd just killed someone else?

"Mr. Reed was under the influence of dangerous, psyche-altering drugs. At the time of his original conviction, his lawyer did not pursue an NGRI defense. However, based on my review and treatment of Mr. Reed, I believe this was a grave injustice. This man is mentally ill and has been since he was ten years old. He has never been treated for his myriad of mental health diagnoses, and Babcock is not set up to deal with prisoners with Mr. Reed's unique health needs. Like anyone, I believe Mr. Reed has the right to appropriate mental healthcare, and I have no doubt in my mind that with proper treatment, he will experience rehabilitation. Therefore, I petition this esteemed board to consider correcting this error as soon as possible," the doctor requested.

Dane stared, unable to believe the words coming out of this woman's mouth. Dane agreed his brother needed help, but not at the risk of him being out in the general public. Transferring his brother to a mental institution would make this world a more dangerous place.

"John Reed, we understand you also had a statement prepared. Is that correct?" the board president asked Dane's brother.

“Yes, ma’am,” he said softly as he stood up, keeping his eyes downcast.

“Go ahead, Mr. Reed,” the board president encouraged in a tone that sounded to Dane like she was talking to a special needs child.

He unfolded a wrinkled piece of paper and began to read in a calm, educated way, as if he’d been coached. “I have served seventeen years of two concurrent life sentences. In that time, I have worked with Dr. Garland and others to understand the magnitude and ramifications of my actions and why I committed these heinous acts of violence. In my first year at Babcock, I successfully completed a drug rehabilitation program, and I've worked with other addicts ever since, trying to help them see how important getting and staying clean is. My addiction made me do things I truly believe I would've never done had I been sober. But I still chose to take drugs. I rejected my parents' many attempts to help me, and I can never course correct the pain or damage I have caused to my family, especially my younger brother," John Reed explained, anguish in his voice.

Dane gritted his teeth. His brother had always been a liar, and Dane believed with every bone in his body – including the ones his brother had broken the night he’d tried to kill him – that he was lying now. Dane shook his head, hoping beyond hope the parole board wasn’t buying it.

The board members listened intently, their faces unreadable. They peppered Dane’s brother with questions, probing for inconsistencies, searching for evidence of genuine remorse and a commitment to change. John appeared to answer each question honestly and forthrightly, his voice unwavering despite the pressure.

“Thank you, Mr. Reed. You may be seated. Before we make our decision, Mr. Wyatt Reed has also requested to be heard. Is there a Mr. Wyatt Reed here today?” the board president called out.

Dane stood up, his confidence fading fast. “Yes, your Honor, that’s me.”

“Mr. Reed, please approach and provide your statement,” the board president stated.

Dane walked to the front hesitantly, terrified to be near his brother. He glanced to where his brother was seated, but his brother’s eyes were still facing the ground.

“When I was twelve years old, my parents gave my brother an ultimatum. They told him he could get help or he could get out. He chose to leave. His absence was devastating to our family, but the drugs and the choices he'd made before he left had been so much worse. He'd stolen from my parents over and over again to pay for drugs and who knows what else. He'd taken things and pawned them for a quick buck, things like jewelry and my great-grandmother's silver, things that could never be replaced. And my parents never recovered them. They were just gone," Dane recounted, his heart pounding in his ears so loudly he believed his brother, across the room, could probably hear it.

"He chose drugs and that lifestyle over our family. Then, in the middle of the night, he broke into our home and viciously attacked my parents with a chef's knife from the butcher block in the kitchen. He stabbed my father seventeen times and my mother twenty-two times. Then, he came after me. The doctors never told me how many times my brother stabbed me, but I had eleven broken bones in addition to however many stab wounds there were."

His voice shook as he talked about his own wounds, knowing there were some scars his brother had left that would never heal. That was something he could not say, something he could not give his brother the satisfaction of knowing. That was his pain and his alone.

"My brother has major issues. My parents tried and failed to get him help. Babcock obviously tried and failed to get him help. All these failures are not an accident—they're a warning. There is no rehabilitation possible with my brother. I don't know Dr. Garland or what her motives are here today, but she's never reached out to me or anyone affected by my brother's monstrous actions to actually understand anyone else's perspective beyond his. I find that reprehensible and concerning. I also feel my brother is a master manipulator, and I fear he is exploiting mental health concerns for his own gain."

Then, Dane added, "I do not believe John Baxter Reed is capable of any kind of rehabilitation, and if you move forward with the doctor's request, the blood of anyone he kills in the future will be on your hands."

"Thank you, Mr. Reed," the board president said, her expression unreadable.

Dane returned to his seat and waited for the verdict. He hoped his impassioned plea to reconsider the doctor's request would be enough, but he worried it wasn't. He watched as the board members deliberated in hushed tones, their faces hidden behind a veil of official neutrality.

Finally, the president spoke again. Her voice remained emotionless, but the words she uttered carried the weight of a life-changing decision. "Mr. John Baxter Reed," she said, "the board has reviewed your case and considered your testimony and the testimony of Dr. Garland and your brother, Wyatt. At this time, the board has decided to grant your doctor's request for immediate transfer to an appropriate mental healthcare facility."

Dane felt the floor give out underneath him as he replayed the board president's words in his head. It didn't make sense. If he'd been standing, he would've fallen flat on his face.

Then, he looked over to where his brother was.

Dr. Garland thanked the parole board members and then whispered something in John's ear as he stood up. Dane watched in horror as his brother walked towards him, his shackles clanging with each shuffling step. John Reed glanced down at his little brother as he passed him by, their similar, brown-eyed stares meeting only for a moment.

It was just long enough for his brother to flash Dane a malicious smirk that spoke his intentions as clearly as if he'd said them aloud.

When I get out, I'm paying you a little visit and finishing what I started.

NOW AVAILABLE!

CAN'T SLEEP
(A Nora Price FBI Suspense Thriller—Book Four)

FBI agent Nora Price is haunted by the childhood memory of being abducted, with her sister, by a notorious serial killer—and escaping, while her sister was never found. Now, ominous tombstones suddenly appear in the front lawns of unsuspecting residents, spelling out the names of homeowners—and next victims—and Nora, while searching for her sister, must race to save them before it's too late….

"This is an excellent book… When you start reading, be sure you don't have to wake up early!"
—Reader review for The Killing Game

CAN'T SLEEP is book #4 in a new series by #1 bestselling mystery and suspense author Kate Bold, whose bestseller NOT ME (a free download) has received over 1,500 five star ratings and reviews.

A page-turning and harrowing crime thriller featuring a brilliant and tortured FBI agent, the NORA PRICE series is a riveting mystery, packed with non-stop action, suspense, twists and turns, revelations, and driven by a breakneck pace that will keep you flipping pages late into the night. Fans of Rachel Caine, Teresa Driscoll, and Robert Dugoni are sure to fall in love.

Future books in the series are now available.

"This book moved very fast and every page was exciting. Plenty of dialogue, you absolutely love the characters, and you were rooting for the good guy throughout the whole story… I look forward to reading the next in the series."
—Reader review for The Killing Game

"Kate did an amazing job on this book and I was hooked from the first chapter!"
—Reader review for The Killing Game

"I really enjoyed this book. The characters were authentic, and I see the bad guys as something we hear about daily on the news... Looking forward to book 2."
—Reader review for The Killing Game

"This was a really good book. The main characters were real, flawed and human. The story went along quickly and wasn't mired in too many unnecessary details. I really enjoyed it."
—Reader review for The Killing Game

"Alexa Chase is headstrong, impatient, but most of all brave with a capital B. She never, repeat never, backs down until the bad guys are put where they belong. Clearly five stars!"
—Reader review for The Killing Game

"Captivating and riveting serial murder with a twist of the macabre… Very well done."
—Reader review for The Killing Game

"WOW what a great read! Talk about a diabolical killer! Really enjoyed this book. Looking forward to reading others by this author as well."
—Reader review for The Killing Game

"Page turner for sure. Great characters and relationships. I got into the middle of this story and couldn't put it down. Looking forward to more from Kate Bold."
—Reader review for The Killing Game

"Hard to put down. It has an excellent plot and has the right amount of suspense. I really enjoyed this book."
—Reader review for The Killing Game

"Extremely well written, and well worth buying and reading. I can't wait to read book two!"

—Reader review for The Killing Game

Kate Bold

Bestselling author Kate Bold is author of the ALEXA CHASE SUSPENSE THRILLER series, comprising six books (and counting); the ASHLEY HOPE SUSPENSE THRILLER series, comprising six books (and counting); the CAMILLE GRACE FBI SUSPENSE THRILLER series, comprising eight books (and counting); the HARLEY COLE FBI SUSPENSE THRILLER series, comprising eleven books (and counting); the KAYLIE BROOKS PSYCHOLOGICAL SUSPENSE THRILLER series, comprising five books (and counting); the EVE HOPE FBI SUSPENSE THRILLER series, comprising seven books (and counting); the DYLAN FIRST FBI SUSPENSE THRILLER series, comprising five books (and counting); the LAUREN LAMB FBI SUSPENSE THRILLER series, comprising five books (and counting); the KELSEY HAWK MYSTERY series, comprising five books (and counting); the NORA PRICE MYSTERY series, comprising five books (and counting); and the NINA VEIL MYSTERY series, comprising five books (and counting).

An avid reader and lifelong fan of the mystery and thriller genres, Kate loves to hear from you, so please feel free to visit www.kateboldauthor.com to learn more and stay in touch.

BOOKS BY KATE BOLD

NINA VEIL MYSTERY
AWAY FROM HERE (Book #1)
AWAY FROM HIM (Book #2)
AWAY FROM HOPE (Book #3)
AWAY FROM HOME (Book #4)
AWAY FROM HUMANITY (Book #5)

NORA PRICE MYSTERY
CAN'T RUN (Book #1)
CAN'T HIDE (Book #2)
CAN'T ESCAPE (Book #3)
CAN'T SLEEP (Book #4)
CAN'T FORGET (Book #5)

KELSEY HAWK MYSTERY
DEAD INSIDE (Book #1)
DEAD RECKONING (Book #2)
DEAD TO ME (Book #3)
DEAD SILENCE (Book #4)
DEAD TO DAWN (Book #5)

ALEXA CHASE SUSPENSE THRILLER
THE KILLING GAME (Book #1)
THE KILLING TIDE (Book #2)
THE KILLING HOUR (Book #3)
THE KILLING POINT (Book #4)
THE KILLING FOG (Book #5)
THE KILLING PLACE (Book #6)

ASHLEY HOPE SUSPENSE THRILLER
LET ME GO (Book #1)
LET ME OUT (Book #2)
LET ME LIVE (Book #3)
LET ME BREATHE (Book #4)

LET ME FORGET (Book #5)
LET ME ESCAPE (Book #6)

CAMILLE GRACE FBI SUSPENSE THRILLER
NOT ME (Book #1)
NOT NOW (Book #2)
NOT WELL (Book #3)
NOT HER (Book #4)
NOT NORMAL (Book #5)
NOT AGAIN (Book #6)
NOT SAFE (Book #7)
NOT TODAY (Book #8)

HARLEY COLE FBI SUSPENSE THRILLER
NOWHERE SAFE (Book #1)
NOWHERE LEFT (Book #2)
NOWHERE TO RUN (Book #3)
NOWHERE LIKE THIS (Book #4)
NOWHERE GIRL (Book #5)
NOWHERE TO HIDE (Book #6)
NOWHERE CERTAIN (Book #7)
NOWHERE PURE (Book #8)
NOWHERE SOUND (Book #9)
NOWHERE SANE (Book #10)
NOWHERE TRUE (Book #11)

KAYLIE BROOKS PYSCHOLOGICAL SUSPENSE THRILLER
LAST BREATH (Book #1)
LAST CHANCE (Book #2)
LAST WISH (Book #3)
LAST SHOT (Book #4)
LAST MISTAKE (Book #5)

EVE HOPE FBI SUSPENSE THRILLER
IN HIS BLOOD (Book #1)
IN HIS SIGHTS (Book #2)
IN HIS REACH (Book #3)
IN HIS MIND (Book #4)
IN HIS WAY (Book #5)

IN HIS THOUGHTS (Book #6)
IN HIS DREAMS (Book #7)

DYLAN FIRST FBI SUSPENSE THRILLER
OUT OF REACH (Book #1)
OUT OF TOUCH (Book #2)
OUT OF TIME (Book #3)
OUT OF BOUNDS (Book #4)
OUT OF LUCK (Book #5)

LAUREN LAMB FBI SUSPENSE THRILLER
SOMETHING KNOCKING (Book #1)
SOMETHING CALLING (Book #2)
SOMETHING WRONG (Book 3)
SOMETHING DARK (Book #4)
SOMETHING TO HIDE (Book #5)

Made in United States
North Haven, CT
26 February 2024

49263493R00087